Island Detective
Sue Brown

Copyright ©2021 Sue Brown
Published by One Hat Press
Cover design by Anna Martin
Formatting by Format4U/Pippa Wood

Skandik and Owens, private detectives. Can they find a man who vanished over thirty years ago? Or will their first case break them apart?

With a new job as a private detective on a small island, Olaf has everything he's dreamed of. A life as an openly gay man, a partner who adores every fuzzy hair on his body, and his adopted family and friends who love him. So why does he feel something is still missing?

With a promotion that's his for the taking, Paul has everything he never dreamed of. His closeted cop is finally in the same country as him. His interfering family and friends are happy for him. So why isn't he satisfied?

Then on his first day of business Olaf gets the worst possible case. To discover whether a sixteen-year-old gay boy who disappeared thirty-five years ago is alive or dead. As they delve into the dark history of the boy's family, both Olaf and Paul are forced to confront their relationship.

Will Paul take the promotion? Will Olaf walk away if he does? Or will they face the fact that their relationship is more important than anything else?

All Rights Are Reserved. No part of this book may be used or reproduced in any manner whatsoever without written permission, except in the case of brief quotations embodied in critical articles and reviews.

This book is a work of fiction. While reference might be made to actual historical events or existing locations, the names, characters, places and incidents are either the product of the author's imagination or are used fictitiously, and any resemblance to actual persons, living or dead, business establishments, events, or locales is entirely coincidental.

Contents

Chapter 1	1
Chapter 2	10
Chapter 3	28
Chapter 4	42
Chapter 5	55
Chapter 6	62
Chapter 7	75
Chapter 8	89
Chapter 9	104
Chapter 10	118
Chapter 11	133
Chapter 12	146
Chapter 13	162
Chapter 14	176
Chapter 15	190
Epilogue	198
Also by Sue Brown	
About Sue Brown	

Chapter 1

Detective Olaf Skandik watched with resignation as the teenager hurled the open carton of meat, vegetables, and sauce straight at him.

What a waste of food.

He stared at the mess on his shirt and jacket as the kids cackled like hyenas, and even his co-workers snickered as they arrested the perpetrator.

"I'm resigning," he announced.

"Sure you are, Skandi," Sergeant Biggs agreed cheerfully, and the other police officers gave him the same tired, cynical grins.

Olaf gritted his teeth. He had never convinced his co-workers to quit calling him Skandi and he wasn't surprised no one believed him. They all threatened it at least twice a week. But watching the Chinese food drip onto the floor, Olaf meant it. He'd had enough. After eighteen years of being a cop, some asshole kid's takeout was the least of it, but it was the straw that broke the camel's back. He was done.

He finished his shift and drove to his empty house, stripped off his ruined suit and shirt, then dressed in a hoodie and old jeans.

His fiancé was back in London, on his own shift

as a Met inspector. Olaf desperately wanted to talk to him, but he knew Paul wouldn't be free for hours. He sent Paul a message.

"Love you."

Then he called the next best thing.

"Hey, Olaf."

The American accent, even muted after years on the island, was like a piece of home. Tears prickled the back of Olaf's eyes.

He forced a smile before he answered. "Hi, Liam."

"What's wrong? Is Paul okay?"

"He's fine—I think." Olaf hesitated, then he said, "Could I come over?"

"Of course. Do you want to eat? We were thinking Chinese."

Unseen, Olaf gave a wry smile. "I think I've had enough Chinese for one day. I'll figure it out myself."

"Okay. See you later."

Olaf crashed on the sofa and closed his eyes. He needed to eat, but it could wait until later. The smell of the Chinese food lingered in his nostrils.

Liam and his husband, Sam, lived in a small one story in a cul-de-sac. It was tiny and still had the same shabby appearance it had when Sam's grandmother lived there, but Olaf liked it. He was going to beg if he could sleep on the couch tonight. He needed to get hammered.

He knocked at the door, unsurprised to hear Liam call out that he would answer it. The door swung open, and a grey-haired man smiled at him, then the smile faded into a frown.

"You look like shit," Liam announced.

Olaf leaned against the door frame. "Thanks."

Liam eyed the beer in Olaf's hands. "Come on in. Was it a bad shift?"

He stood back to let Olaf in through the door. Liam was one of Olaf's closest friends. Both American, they were a similar age. Both in love with an impossible Owens boy. The first time Olaf had met him, Liam had been lying in a hospital bed in a coma, barely recognisable. Olaf had also met the man who would change his life forever. If he'd known what he was getting into when he agreed to meet two English guys looking for a missing boyfriend...he would probably have run in the opposite direction.

"I quit," Olaf blurted out before Liam had shut the door.

"Bloody hell, Skandik. What the hell did you do that for?" Sam, Liam's husband, appeared in the kitchen doorway.

As ever, Olaf felt the desperate need for Paul when he saw Sam. The two brothers looked more alike than ever as they grew older, with dark blond hair and deep brown eyes. Now in their mid-thirties, Sam looked less like a hippie surfer and Paul less like an eighties reject. On the quiet, Olaf and Liam confessed to each other they both missed those early days.

"A kid threw a carton of noodles at me."

"You quit your job because a kid threw food at you?" Liam asked cautiously.

Olaf sighed. It sounded stupid, but, "Yeah."

Liam wrapped an arm around his shoulders and led him into the living room, pushing him into what used to be Rose's armchair. They'd decorated all the rooms since they'd lived there, but neither of them had felt it was right to get rid of her chair.

"Sit down, drink a beer, and talk," Liam said.

Olaf stared at the can of beer and wondered what he could say that would make any sense. It wasn't helped by Liam and Sam sat opposite him, curled around each other like puppies in a pile. Once again, Olaf's heart ached with loneliness.

"Olaf?" Liam prompted.

He sighed and looked at his friends. "It wasn't just the food. I've been thinking about it for a while. Since I got residency." When confirmation came through that he could stay in the country, it was as if a switch had been flicked in his head. He didn't want to be a cop anymore. But he'd carried on because leaving the police force was one thing, but what the hell else could he do? He didn't want to end up dependent on Paul for money. Not that he had to, because he had savings and his family was wealthy, but he hadn't asked them for help in years.

"What are you going to do?" Liam asked as if he'd read Olaf's mind.

"I want to be a PI."

The idea came like a bolt out of the blue.

Sam wrinkled his brow. "A private investigator? But isn't that what you're doing now?"

"I want to be able to choose my cases and the hours I work." Olaf grimaced as he admitted something he'd never said out loud before. "I'm forty-five. I'm not going to get promoted now. I was thinking of leaving the police when I first met you, as my partner was retiring, but she stayed on. And then I needed a job that would allow me to be over here while Paul and I decided what we were gonna do. I've been in the military and the police. Now I want a slower pace."

Sam didn't look convinced. "But this is the Isle of Wight, Olaf. You're going to be finding lost dogs and chasing cheating husbands."

"Unless you're going up to London. There'll be more work up there," Liam suggested.

Olaf knew that, but he really didn't want to live in London. He and Paul spent weekends at each other's homes, but Paul preferred to come to the island, and Olaf was fine with that. "I can start here, and if I get no work, then maybe I'll move to London."

"Have you spoken to Paul about it?" Sam asked.

"No." Olaf ran a hand over his short-cropped hair. "I haven't seen him for months because of the lockdown. And when I talk to him, we're—" he coughed "—otherwise engaged."

Liam sighed. "Olaf, you've got to try talking occasionally."

Olaf blushed, but Sam chuckled. "They are talking. Just not with their mouths."

"Gross." Liam pulled a face.

"But he's right," Olaf admitted. "Talking isn't the main thing on our minds."

"This is your chance to live with Paul," Liam said gently.

"But I love it here. I hate Paul's apartment. I can't breathe there. And there's you guys. You're my friends."

"Are we more important than Paul?"

"Stab me in the heart, why don't you?" Olaf growled.

"You're both so stubborn," Sam muttered. "One of you is going to have to compromise."

"And you think that should be me—again."

"I think you need to decide what's more important to you," Liam said.

"You think Paul isn't important to me? I travelled halfway around the world to be with him."

"Except you aren't, are you?" Sam pointed out. "You live here, and he lives in London. And you both hate it."

"What did he compromise on?" Olaf snarled.

Sam's eyes narrowed, but he said calmly, "Paul never touched another man or woman after he met you. My brother was a manwhore. But he thought you were worth it."

This was so frustrating. Olaf hated the fact they were right. He rubbed his temples, feeling the pressure headache start to build. Maybe he should go home before he said something he'd regret.

Sam got to his feet. "I'll make tea."

He vanished into the kitchen, leaving Liam staring worriedly at Olaf.

"He's going to call Paul, isn't he?" Olaf asked, resigned to an Owens family intervention.

"Paul, Mattie, Cam, and Nick," Liam agreed. "Or maybe Logan."

"I don't need a shrink," Olaf growled.

Liam frowned at him. "You need friends. That's what we are."

"What do I do?" Olaf knew he sounded pathetic. Then his phone buzzed in his pocket, and he pulled it out and looked at the screen.

"CALL ME NOW!"

"Shit! What did Sam say to him?"

"I'll go and help Sam." Liam scurried out of the room.

Coward.

Olaf tapped in Paul's number.

"What the hell have you just done?" Paul barked.

"Sam called you."

"Sam. Tea. Biggsy. Howler. Roper. Jonesy... I've got fifteen messages on my phone just from your colleagues. You've freaked out the entire nick. Even the inspector called me. What's going on?"

"I resigned," Olaf said.

"I know that, babe," Paul said, his voice calmer now. "But why?"

"A kid threw Chinese food on me." It still sounded pathetic when Olaf said it out loud.

"You resigned because a kid threw food at you."

"Yes. No. Kinda."

Paul huffed in his ear. "Olaf, do you even know why you resigned?"

"I've been thinking about it for a while," he admitted.

He could feel Paul's hurt even through the phone.

"You didn't say anything to me."

"I know."

"Why not?"

Olaf sighed. "Because my head's a mess and we spend so little time together, I didn't want to waste time asking you to deal with my shit."

Paul gave a bark of laughter. "So instead you wait for a flying kebab to hit you before you resign."

"Chinese," Olaf corrected.

"Whatever." Paul obviously dismissed it as unimportant.

"I need a beer."

Olaf stood and went into the kitchen to find Liam and Sam leaning against the kitchen counter, kissing. And not the peck on the cheek you'd give your auntie. He suddenly remembered Paul moaning about them when he first met them all.

"Is this a kissing book?" he muttered and backed out of the kitchen.

"What?" Paul sounded confused.

"Never mind. Have you finished your shift?"

"Not yet. I'm covering for someone for a couple of hours. I ought to go."

Olaf suddenly felt exhausted, needing to go home. "Call me when you get home?"

"It'll be late," Paul warned.

"I don't care. I just want to say goodnight to you."

"I'll call you," Paul promised. "Olaf?"

"Hmm?"

"What are you going to do?"

Olaf could hear the tension in Paul's voice.

"I want to become a private investigator."

"On the island?"

"I think so," Olaf admitted.

"You're not flying home?" Paul asked.

"I *am* home, babe. I don't want to live anywhere else."

"Thank God."

Now the relief was obvious. Olaf smiled to himself. They may still be a hundred miles and a ferry ride apart, but they were still partners-in-crime.

"Guv, you're needed in the custody suite."

Not Paul's voice, but Paul sighed. "I've—"

"Got to go. I know. I'll talk to you later."

Olaf stared at his phone after they disconnected. He should have spoken to Paul sooner.

"Is he still talking to you?" Liam asked.

He and Sam stood in the doorway, mouths puffy and eyes glazed.

Olaf really needed to go home. He could still drive. He smiled at them, trying not to let his heartache show. They deserved their happiness. "He is. I need to sleep. Keep the beer."

Liam came forwards and wrapped his arms around Olaf. "You'll be a great PI."

Sam smirked at them both. "How many dick jokes is Paul going to find?"

Olaf groaned. He hadn't thought of that. "Maybe he'll miss the joke."

"This is Paul we're talking about. My little brother. He's *always* going to find a dick joke."

"Good point," Olaf said glumly.

Chapter 2

Sunday

"Look at my man. A Private Dick."

Paul Owens smirked as he studied the door.

Olaf Skandik.

Private Investigator.

Olaf rolled his eyes. "You had to get a dick joke in there somewhere, didn't you?"

"Well duh. Did you expect anything different?"

"I expected it sooner," Olaf admitted, admiring his name on the door.

Paul raised his eyebrow. "Are you going to open the door or are we going to spend all day staring at the sign?"

Olaf huffed as he fumbled with the key. His hands shook as he made a second attempt to get the key in the lock.

"Let me do it," Paul suggested.

But rather than taking the key from him, Paul placed his hands over Olaf's and guided the key in. It turned like a charm.

"I don't know why I'm so nervous," Olaf admitted.

Paul pushed the door open. "This is the start of your new life, babe. Olaf Skandik, private detective. Finder of lost dogs and cheating husbands."

Olaf had a horrible feeling he was right.

They surveyed the small office, barely large enough for a desk and a chair.

"It's...compact," Paul said diplomatically.

"It's all I can afford at the moment."

He'd been lucky that the offices were still empty above the Blue Lagoon restaurant. He wasn't sure about having Wig and Nibs as his friends and landlords, but at least there was an endless supply of coffee downstairs.

"You know you can never complain about my flat again," Paul said with undisguised glee.

Olaf gave a resigned sigh. "I know."

He'd contemplated working from home, but he didn't want clients knowing where he lived. This office, barely larger than a shoebox, was all he could afford until he was established, unless he asked his parents for money. Which was never going to happen.

"It's very beige."

His landlords, Wig and Nibs had decorated the room in neutral colours, but Paul was right. It was beige.

"But it's all yours."

Olaf turned to see Paul grinning at him, and the warmth of his smile sent a message straight to his dick. He pushed the door shut with one foot and raised an eyebrow.

"Bend over the desk," he ordered.

Paul's smile went from warm and happy to heated need. "You want to christen the desk?"

He was head down, ass up, before Olaf had

time to say, "I do."

Olaf grinned. His boy never mucked about.

He slid his hands under Paul's sweater, tugging at the T-shirt so he could reach the warm skin beneath.

Paul flinched. "Christ, you could have warmed your hands up, you bastard."

"I am warming them up. On your back," Olaf pointed out, totally unrepentant for the goosebumps under his fingertips.

"It's a good thing I like you," Paul grumbled.

Olaf bent over him to whisper in his ear. "Oh, I think you do more than like me, Mr Owens."

Paul scoffed in the back of his throat, but the shiver told a different story. "Get on with it. I haven't got all day."

Olaf grinned. His boy was all mouth. For a man with no patience, he could be reduced to a boneless heap when Olaf took things slow. They'd been together for eight years—on and off, and, okay, maybe more off than on in the earlier stages—but they'd always come together with clashing need. Making love to Paul Owens was still at the top of Olaf's things-to-do list.

"Earth to Olaf. Are you on the same planet as me?"

Olaf blinked and smiled apologetically at his lover. "Uh...yeah. Sorry. I was thinking."

Paul sighed, turning so he could sit on the desk. "Is it the new job?"

"What?"

"You've been quiet all day. Are you worried about the new job?"

Olaf shook his head. "No." At Paul's frankly sceptical look, he said, "Maybe a little, but it was time, you know? I've been a police officer for nearly twenty years. I was a Marine before that. Now it's time for something different."

He knew Paul wasn't worried about Olaf's change in career. They'd discussed it long and hard. Olaf had residency now, and he'd worked out his finances with Paul's brother, Sam, who despite being a soppy bastard (Paul's words), was a kick-ass accountant. Olaf had made sure he was covered financially for a year before he'd handed in his resignation to the island police force. He'd dotted the i's and crossed the t's.

"So what's wrong?" Paul asked.

"I love you," Olaf blurted out.

"I know that." Paul looked pleased, but still confused. "I love you too."

Olaf drew Paul into his embrace and held him tight. All the words he couldn't say were like a blockage in his throat.

"You're starting to freak me out," Paul said, his mouth pressed against Olaf's Adam's apple.

In truth, Olaf was starting to freak himself out.

Paul tugged Olaf down so that they were staring into each other's face. "Just say whatever it is that's bothering you. We can sort it. You know that."

"Why won't you marry me?"

The second the words were out, Olaf wished he'd kept his mouth shut. He felt Paul still and pull away from him.

"Not this again."

"This again." All Olaf wanted was a straight answer. All he got was deflection.

Paul huffed. "You know why."

"That's the problem. I don't," Olaf said. "We've been engaged for five years. I thought we'd eventually tie the knot."

"Why is it so important to you?" Paul demanded.

"Because I love you and want to call you my husband."

Paul's frustrated expression eased for a second. "It'll happen someday. Can't you be happy with that?"

"Paul, we're not married. We don't live together. I could go home and nothing much would change." He saw Paul's eyes widen. "I'm not going home."

"I thought this *was* your home," Paul said icily, waving a hand around the empty office. "Otherwise, what is all this for?"

He'd managed to do it again. Deflect the questions away from himself and onto Olaf.

Olaf pinched the bridge of his nose, feeling the start of a headache beginning to build. "Forget it. Let's go home."

Paul looked regretfully at the desk, but he stood. "Olaf—"

They both jumped at the knock on the door.

"Are you expecting anyone?" Paul asked.

"No." Olaf had only just gotten the keys. "I have no idea who it could be."

"Well, open the door and find out."

The room was so small Olaf just had to lean

over and turn the handle. A balding middle-aged man, maybe around Olaf's age, smiled nervously at them.

"Mr Skandik?"

"That's me," Olaf said. He stood and saw the guy flinch. Inwardly he sighed. He knew he was tall, and over the years he'd packed on muscle rather than get soft. But he didn't want to scare away his clients, particularly his first. He held out his hand. "Olaf Skandik. How can I help you, Mr...?"

"Sargent. Keith Sargent."

Sargent's handshake was on the limp side, but Olaf could see he was unnerved.

"Paul, would you get a coffee for me and whatever Mr Sargent wants."

Paul scowled but to Olaf's relief, he nodded and looked at Sargent. "What can I get you?"

"Oh...uh...tea, white with two, please."

As Paul left the room, Sargent said, "Is Paul your secretary?"

Olaf heard Paul's snort before the door closed. He was never going to live that down.

"Paul is my fiancé."

He waited for a reaction, but instead Sargent seemed... what? Relieved? If he had to put an emotion on it, he would say relieved.

"Please, take a seat, Mr Sargent." Olaf pointed at the chair in front of his desk. "I've only just got the keys to my office."

Sargent sat and looked around. "Am I your first client?"

Olaf nodded. "You are, but not my first

investigation. I'm...I was...a detective."

He'd expected the reassurance to allay Sargent's worries but instead he received a frown.

"A cop?" Sargent said the words as if they left a nasty taste in his mouth.

"Yes."

"Why did you leave?"

"I wanted something different," Olaf said. He didn't need to be telling the client his motivation, but it felt good to say it out loud. "What can I do for you?"

Sargent hesitated, then he said, "I need you to find someone."

"Who?"

Olaf realised he didn't even have a notepad and pen to make notes. The desk wasn't stocked yet. But he pulled out his phone. He could make notes on that for now.

"My brother." Sargent stared at his hands, seemingly lost in thought.

Olaf had learned over the years that jumping in with questions wasn't always the way to get the information he wanted. He waited until Sargent looked up.

"My brother vanished thirty-five years ago. June 1986. Bobby was sixteen. He left home one night and never returned."

"On the island?"

"Yes."

"What do *you* think happened to him?" Olaf asked.

"I think my father killed him," Sargent said harshly. "I want you to find him and prove me wrong."

So much for finding lost dogs and cheating husbands.

"What happens if I find your father did murder him?"

Sargent shrugged. "It's too late now. The old bastard died last week."

In the uncomfortable silence, Paul walked in with a tray with three take out cups, a pen, and a notepad under one arm.

Olaf smiled at him gratefully. "Thanks, Paul."

"You're welcome." Paul glanced at Sargent who'd gone back to staring at his hands, and then back to Olaf.

"Missing brother," Olaf mouthed.

"I'll leave you to it."

Sargent looked up at Paul. "Are you a detective too?"

Paul shook his head. "Met police. Inspector."

It was hard to miss Sargent's sneer.

"You don't like the police?" Olaf asked. He was proud of being a cop. Typical that his first client would be a cop hater.

"My dad was a policeman," Sargent muttered. "You can imagine how much effort the local cops made to find my brother."

Olaf jumped as Paul clicked his fingers.

"Your brother was called Bobby?"

Sargent, who'd also jumped, looked surprised. "He was. Robert Sargent. I'm surprised you remember the case. You're too young to have been in the police force then."

"Not many people go missing from the island.

Cops still talk about him."

They do?

Olaf had worked for the Island force for five years and hadn't heard about the case. But then Paul had been on the island a lot longer than him.

"Oh? What do they think happened?" Sargent snarled.

Paul looked down at his angry face. "Bobby was gay, wasn't he?"

Sargent gave a curt nod. "No one ever told me to my face. I was just a kid. But I heard the rumours."

"And your dad didn't approve."

Olaf wondered if *he* should be the one asking the questions, but it gave him a chance to observe Keith Sargent.

"My dad hated queers. I think Bobby tried to hide it from him, he was too..." Sargent was obviously trying to find the right language.

"We understand," Olaf said quietly.

Sargent gave him a grateful smile. "My dad knew. He told me Bobby ran away to find other...gays."

Paul nodded. "But you don't believe him."

"No, I don't. He was easier to live with when Bobby was gone. Less...violent. Like he knew Bobby was never going to come back."

"What do you think happened to him?" Olaf asked.

"I think my dad killed him and dumped his body out at sea. He had a dinghy."

Well, that was blunt enough.

"I can look for your brother, but it's been

thirty-five years," Olaf said. "If I do find out he's dead, are you sure you can handle that news?"

Sargent turned to face him. "It's better than not knowing. I loved my brother, Mr Skandik. He deserves to come home."

"What happens if he's alive and doesn't want to 'come home'?"

"Then I'll know he's alive. And if he's happy that's worth knowing too."

Olaf nodded. Next problem. What did he charge for a thirty-five-year-old cold case with little chance of success?

As if he'd read his mind Sargent reached into his pocket and pulled out a cheque.

"I hope this is enough for a down payment."

Olaf looked at it and nearly choked. Ten thousand pounds. Paul leaned over and plucked the cheque out of Olaf's fingers.

"I'll put that in the bank on my way home."

Olaf was going to have to have a serious talk with his fiancé about interfering in his business.

"That's a large amount on something that could end with little success," Olaf warned.

Sargent gave an indifferent shrug. "It's not my money. It's my dad's. I don't want his blood money. I want my brother."

Olaf breathed easier. "I'll do my best to find him."

"We both will," Paul promised.

There was a note in Paul's voice that made Olaf suspicious, but Paul's attention was focused on Sargent, who had sat back in his chair looking far more relaxed than when he'd walked in, his face less pinched around the eyes and mouth.

"My wife thinks I'm wasting my money. She wants to spend it on a caravan," Sargent admitted.

Olaf thought his wife probably had a point.

But Paul said, "Family is important."

Sargent nodded in agreement. "She'll get her caravan. I love Miriam, and I want to keep the peace. But if Bobby's alive I want him to know I never forgot about him. I also want to know why he never came home."

"Why did you wait this long?" Olaf asked.

"Dad only died last month. The bastard hung on until he was nearly ninety." Sargent got to his feet. "I've got to get back to work."

Olaf stood and shook his hand. "How did you find me?"

"Chrissie Owens. She runs the pub?" At Olaf's nod, Sargent said, "I deliver for a local brewery. We got talking this morning, and I told her about my brother. She said one of her in-laws was a private detective. She gave me this address."

Olaf sighed. Paul was grinning like a lunatic. The Owenses struck again. Of course, one of them had to stick their nose in.

He pulled out his wallet and fished out a business card. "Take my card, Mr Sargent. It's got my phone number and email."

"Call me Keith. Mr Sargent was my dad, and I don't want to be reminded of him."

"I'll walk you down, Keith," Paul said. "Olaf has got work to do." He leaned forwards and kissed Olaf on the cheek. Keith didn't seem to care.

The room seemed much larger without the

other two men in it. Olaf sat down behind his desk and looked at the blank pad of paper. He'd failed to make a single note while his client was there.

He pulled the pad towards him and started to write. Anything he couldn't remember, Paul would know. Paul never forgot anything. Olaf had learned that to his cost.

A gay man missing for thirty-five years. Possibly murdered by his cop father. What a first case for his new career.

When Olaf had written everything he could remember, he decided he needed more coffee. He went downstairs and into the restaurant.

Wig eyed him carefully. "You look shell-shocked."

"I am," Olaf admitted. "I've gotten my first client."

"That was fast. I thought you weren't open for business yet."

"I'm not. At least, I wasn't. I guess now I am."

Wig rolled his eyes at Olaf's babble. "Go and sit down, and I'll bring you coffee."

"Thanks."

Olaf smiled at him gratefully and headed to a free table in the corner of the restaurant. The Blue Lagoon had undergone a significant transformation since Olaf's first visit. It was three times the size, for one thing. He was pleased to see how busy the place was, despite the tourist season starting late because of the latest lockdown. Wig and Nibs had kept the place going with takeaways. Nibs's breakfasts were legendary, but the strain had started to show.

"Skiving already?" Liam asked, placing the coffee in front of him.

Olaf smiled at him. "I've gotten my first case."

Liam's smile lit up his face. "Go you. I thought you weren't open yet."

"I'm not officially. But he turned up on the doorstep as I showed Paul the office. Chrissie sent him my way."

"Please tell me your client didn't catch you bending Paul over the desk."

That was the problem with being part of the Owens family. Everyone knew your business. He would not blush.

"I thought you weren't working here anymore?" Olaf said, pleased at how steady his voice sounded.

Liam was in the middle of a philosophy degree. He'd been a technical writer but after being at the wrong end of a hit and run, he'd found the work beyond him. He'd struggled to find something to do, but finally he'd admitted he'd always wanted to go to college. With the money from the accident allowing him to go back to school, he enrolled and found himself in a classroom full of teenagers. First of all, he'd been ready to bolt. Now he loved it.

Liam smirked at him. "Nice deflection."

"You noticed, huh?"

"In answer to your question, Wig is short a waiter this week, so he asked me to step in. I've finished my classes for the year. I've just got assignments to finish up. Sam's just happy I'm out from under his feet."

Olaf was sure Sam would prefer to have his husband on the end of a leash where he could see him. Sam had serious co-dependency issues where Liam was concerned.

"Gotta go," Liam muttered as Wig called his name. "The bingo crowd is in soon. Wig is in princess mode."

Olaf groaned. "I'm out of here."

"You know they love you."

"They keep pinching my ass," Olaf protested. "I come home with a butt full of bruises, and Paul gets annoyed."

"You keep telling yourself that," Liam said.

Wig yelled for Liam again, his tone having a distinct edge. The manager of the Blue Lagoon did not like to be kept waiting.

Olaf smiled as Liam hurried off.

"More coffee?" Wig asked, appearing at his side.

"How long have I got before the old girls arrive?"

Wig craned to look at the clock. "Ten minutes."

"I'm going." He pulled out his wallet.

"On the house. Paul said you're finding a missing gay man."

"Paul has a big mouth," Olaf muttered. Wig opened his mouth and Olaf held up his hand. "No, I don't want to hear whatever sexual innuendo you're about to make."

"What makes you think—" Wig protested.

"I *know* you."

"He's got you there," Liam agreed as he joined them. "The ladies are getting off the bus. Go out the back way."

Wig smirked at them both. "Coward."

"Butt. Bruises. Hurt," Olaf complained.

He ignored the two men snickering behind him as he headed for the back door leading to Wig and Nibs's flat. Middle-aged men should not get their butts pinched by elderly women who should know better. Even if he did know them all by name and did their shopping when they needed help.

He sat in his car and looked at his notes. First, he needed to call his lover.

"How's your bum?"

Olaf sighed at Paul's greeting. "You could have warned me it was bingo day."

"Where would be the fun in that?"

There wasn't much he could answer to that, so he got down to business. "Who would I talk to on the force who isn't going to tell me to fuck off?"

"About Sargent senior?"

"Yeah."

"I've been thinking about that. They're all long retired now. They were a close-knit bunch, and most of them had views similar to Sargent's. You're going to have to handle this carefully."

"Couldn't I get a cheating husband instead?"

"Sorry, lover, this one had to come to you." Paul did sound genuinely sincere.

"Yes, I suppose it did. I wish Rose was still with us. She would know who to talk to."

"She would," Paul said.

Olaf cursed himself for putting the sad note in his lover's voice. The Owens clan deeply missed the matriarch of the family years after her death.

"What about talking to Cam's parents first?" Paul suggested. "They've lived on the island all their lives and they're a similar age to Keith Sargent."

"Good idea. Do you think Jim might know them?"

"See. You're thinking like a detective already. And yes, Dad knows everyone."

"Ha ha," Olaf said sourly.

Paul chuckled and Olaf couldn't help smiling in response.

An elderly woman walking past the car gave him a suspicious stare, then suddenly smiled at him. He waved, recognising her as one of the newer members of the bingo coven.

"I put the cheque in the bank," Paul said. "That caused a flutter. Ten to one they all think Mrs Sargent is having a wild affair with the postman."

Olaf groaned. "Is this what it's going to be like from now on? All innuendo and gossip."

"My sweet summer child, how have you got to your advanced age and not learned the world runs on gossip?"

"You should be the one doing this job."

"I should," Paul agreed. "I'd be awesome at it."

That reminded Olaf that Paul was leaving him again. It would be weeks before he'd see him, as Paul was about to do nights. Olaf hated the idea of being alone. They'd spent most of the previous year apart because of lockdown. Now, with each separation, Olaf wondered when he'd see Paul. Would it be weeks or months?

"Where are you now?"

"At home. I've got to pack before I meet Sam for a drink. Then I'll see you at home for dinner at five."

Olaf gritted his teeth, holding back the accusation that Paul was running away—again. There was no point. They would waste valuable time arguing when all he wanted to do was tie Paul to the bed and never let him go. Maybe Sam wasn't the only one with co-dependency issues.

"Olaf, I—"

"I'll see you later," Olaf said, and disconnected the call before he begged Paul to stay. He threw his phone on the dashboard and sat back in the seat.

Dammit!

Not for the first time, Olaf thought about going back to Kelder. Seeing if he could get his old job back. He was a forty-five-year-old man, and he really wanted his mom. But he loved Paul, and he didn't want to step back into that tightly locked closet. What the hell was he going to do?

Olaf stared bleakly at Sandown pier. He could be on a plane tomorrow. But he'd made a promise. "I'll find Bobby Sargent. Then maybe I'll go." Maybe.

Chapter 3

Sunday

When he was sure Paul had left to meet Sam, Olaf nipped home to pick up his laptop and raided the house for more stationery and a spider plant to make the room less bare. He'd already made a list of things to buy for the office. His coffee machine and small refrigerator were on order.

He headed back to the office, via a coffee shop, to start his research. He could have done the research at home in more comfort, but he didn't want to risk running into Paul until he was ready. He ignored his lizard brain mocking him for being a coward.

Paul had made a good point. He was a damn good detective. This was a case like any other. He'd found missing people before. He'd found Liam. Yes, it was a cold case, but he could find Bobby Sargent, dead or alive.

He'd drink his coffee and use the café Wi-Fi to research Bobby's disappearance. He didn't expect to find much, and he was right. Thirty minutes later Olaf stared at a cached front page of the island paper.

Policeman's son vanishes.

Olaf looked at the grainy photos of Bobby Sargent and the family. He was a handsome boy on the verge of manhood. His eyes sparkled and he had a ready smile. Unlike his father. Even in the family photo he looked grim. Keith was a boy, and he had that ready smile too. Olaf thought of the grim man in his office not two hours before. Had his brother's disappearance beaten the fun out of him? Both boys looked more like their mother than their father. What had happened to her? Keith hadn't mentioned her. Olaf made a note on his pad. He read the text. It was little more than the bare bones of the story. No mention that Bobby was gay, of course.

The only other thing he found was a Facebook page, obviously run by Keith Sargent begging for news about his brother, updated every year on his birthday and June 30th, the day he went missing. Olaf felt singularly sad as he scrolled through the increasingly desperate posts without a single reply. Bobby remained forever sixteen in the photos. Who would recognise him now?

Olaf scrolled down his contacts and found Cam's number.

"Olaf? Is Paul all right?" Cam sounded frantic, over the noise of the garage where he worked.

Olaf sighed. He'd never called Cam during work hours before. "Paul's fine. I'm fine. Climb off the ledge. Listen, I've got my first PI case."

"Hey, congratulations. So why are you calling me?"

"It's a cold case, and I'd like to talk to your parents. They've lived on the island all their lives."

"Sure, I'll send you Mum's number."

Olaf could hear the curiosity in Cam's voice. "Thanks, Cam. I'll tell you more when I see you."

He said goodbye and hesitated. Then he messaged Sergeant Biggs, one of his former co-workers on the island police force. His phone rang five minutes later.

"Desperate to come back already, Skandi?"

Olaf rolled his eyes. "Never. Hey, have you ever heard of Bobby Sargent?" The silence was so long he checked to see if the call had dropped. "Biggsy?"

"Is this your case?"

"Yes."

"Don't touch this one, Olaf. Run away from it."

"You know the case?"

"We all do. Bobby's dad was one of us."

Olaf ignored the implication that he wasn't, even though he'd worked with them for years. "Keith Sargent came to my office. He wants me to find Bobby—dead or alive."

Biggs sighed. "God, I wish he'd let it rest."

"Would you? If it were your brother?"

"I guess not." Biggs huffed, before saying, "Listen, Skandi, cops have long memories, and they're not going to want to dishonour one of their own."

"Even if he killed his own son?" Olaf said sharply.

Biggs was silent for a long moment. Olaf waited him out. "Talk to John Parkin. He worked with the sarge. He's also a friend of the Owens family."

Olaf wrote his name on the notebook. "Where

can I find him?"

"He spends most days in the Royal Oak."

"Thanks, Biggsy."

"Just go easy, yeah? The lads like you, but you don't want to lose their goodwill. Even being Paul Owens's squeeze won't save you if this goes tits up."

Olaf grimaced at the idea. Not one of them. He'd always known his acceptance was largely based on being part of the Owens clan, but he'd hoped he had proved himself as a good cop too. Now it seemed the acceptance was only skin-deep.

The next call was easier. Cam's mum, Charley, was delighted to talk to him, and she knew the family well. He declined an invite to lunch, despite the fact Charley cooked like a dream, and arranged to visit her in the morning. Olaf was fond of Cam's parents. Like Paul's, they smothered all the guys with love whether they wanted it or not. It was easier to go with the flow. At least Charley didn't have an issue with him being a cop—former cop—unlike Mattie, Paul's mom.

His stomach growled and Olaf remembered he hadn't eaten lunch. He looked at the time on his phone and blinked. It was almost five. No wonder he was hungry. He needed to go home and make the most of his limited time with Paul. As if on cue, he received a message.

"Indian or fish and chips?"

Olaf couldn't help giving a rueful smile. This was typical Paul code for 'I'm not going to waste time cooking when you could be banging my brains out.'

He tapped in a quick reply. *"Whatever."*

"Helpful."

Olaf grinned as he stood, rolling his shoulders, and stretching his back. He was getting old.

Paul was curled up on the sofa asleep, knees drawn up to his chest. Olaf studied him for a moment, noticing the lines of tension around his eyes and mouth. He walked over and kissed him on the cheek.

"Um." Paul turned his face, seeking Olaf's mouth.

Olaf sat down and picked Paul up and put him in his lap. There were times it was useful to be taller and more muscled than his partner.

Paul snuggled into him, tucking his head under Olaf's chin. "Food is ordered," he mumbled. "Got to pick it up in thirty minutes."

Olaf held him tighter. "I'll do it. You stay here and snooze."

"Okay." Paul pressed a kiss against his Adam's apple.

Olaf was content to stay where he was, holding his lover. They were silent for several minutes, breathing in unison.

"I hate that I've got to leave again," Paul murmured.

"I could just tie you to the bed."

Paul snorted. "I'd like to point out that you're the one who likes being tied up whilst I ride you until you forget your own name."

This was true. Olaf couldn't argue with that.

"I'll have more time to visit you now," he said, trying to soothe Paul, but really he was trying to soothe the hurt inside him.

Paul raised his head and the pain in his expression made Olaf's heart ache. "We've got to talk."

"Okay," Olaf said warily.

Paul sat up and knuckled his eyes. "God, I'm tired."

As much as Olaf just wanted to get the damn conversation over with, this was not the time. "We're not going to talk now. I need to pick up the curry and you need to finish packing."

"I'd forgotten about the takeaway," Paul admitted.

Olaf got to his feet, aware of Paul's gaze fixed on his exposed belly, his T-shirt riding up as he stretched. It didn't matter what was going on, the spark between them was electric and constant. He had never felt like this about any man before.

Paul licked his lips.

"Oh no." Olaf backed away towards the door. "Not if I'm picking up the takeout."

"Just one lick," Paul begged.

"No," Olaf said firmly, knowing just one lick would become just one suck, which would turn into a blowjob and him pounding Paul into the mattress. "Food."

Paul pouted, jutting out his bottom lip. Olaf grinned and fled, before Paul got his own way. They'd lost more than one takeout because he couldn't resist Paul.

"Coward," Paul yelled after him.

Olaf grinned as he picked up his keys and wallet. Prudent, not cowardly.

Olaf burped after he swallowed the last of his curry.

"Gross," Paul muttered and belched too. He put his plate on the table and sat back. "I needed that."

"Feeling better?" Olaf asked as he stacked his bowl on top of the plates. He'd been hoping for leftovers, but they'd eaten every last scrap of food even though Paul seemed to order for six. He hadn't really eaten all day, and neither had Paul, as Olaf discovered when he pressed him. Paul had a habit of forgetting to eat unless Olaf reminded him, then wondering why he was cranky. Paul would never actually admit he was cranky, despite everyone telling him.

Paul sat back, rubbing his belly. "Yeah."

"Do you want to talk now?"

"Not really, but I need to know. Are you leaving me?" At Olaf's hesitation, Paul sighed. "I guess that's my answer."

"No," Olaf said hastily, grabbing Paul's hand as he stood.

Paul raised an eyebrow. "No?" At least he didn't try to pull away.

"What made you think I was leaving you?"

"You've been looking at flights back to Kelder."

Damn, he should remember to clear his browser history.

"Only for a visit," he said, not sure whether it was the whole truth. From Paul's frown, he didn't seem convinced either. "I was homesick. I want to see Mom and Dad. It's been too long since I last saw them. Now I'm working for myself it'll be easier to go."

"You don't want me to come with you?" Paul sounded hurt, but his expression had eased when Olaf admitted his homesickness.

"I know you don't like the way Mom treats you, and we were gonna save your vacation to go away when everything opened up."

From the way Paul pressed his lips together, it sounded like a lame excuse to him too.

"Convenient."

"Paul, I'm not leaving you," Olaf insisted. "I just need time with my family."

"I thought I was your family."

"I thought so too, but you still don't want to marry me."

Paul tugged his hand away. "Not that again."

Olaf clenched his jaw. What the hell did he have to do to make Paul understand how much this was hurting him?

"Even if we got married, would you come and live in London with me?" Olaf hesitated and Paul gave a curt nod. "I thought not."

"I like it here."

"And you hate London." It wasn't a question. Paul knew the answer well enough.

Olaf nodded. "And you won't transfer to the island."

Also not a question. Paul had always said he'd rather die than transfer. He was a big city cop.

"I've been offered a promotion," Paul said.

Olaf stared at him. "What?"

"Well, more the fast track to promotion if I take the sideways move."

Olaf narrowed his eyes. He would deal later with the fact Paul hadn't told him. They had both been keeping secrets. "You don't sound that happy about it."

"It's into the Major Investigations Team."

This was a big deal. Paul should have been screaming around the house in excitement, rather than the pinched unhappy expression he wore.

"Go on."

"The abused and trafficked children's unit."

"Oh hell, no!" Olaf exploded, standing to face his lover.

Suddenly it all became clear. Paul's pinched expression. The secrecy.

"If I take the job, I'll get a fast track to Chief Inspector."

"Why you?" Olaf demanded.

"Because I'm a damn good cop," Paul said bleakly.

"No. Why do they want you in that unit?"

"Because of the Fryer case. They remember me. I may have been a beat copper, but I cracked the case."

"That was years ago."

Paul shrugged. "I kept in touch with some of the guys."

"That case nearly killed you, Paul," Olaf pointed out. He was furious at Paul for even considering it.

"It wasn't *that* bad."

Olaf glared at Paul, who refused to meet his

gaze. "Do you remember that time? You broke up with me. Refused to take my calls. I was collateral damage in that fucking awful case."

He'd been ready to walk away at that point. If it hadn't been for the interventions of Paul's family and their interfering friends, he would have called it quits.

"You broke up with me, arsehole," Paul snarled.

Olaf waved a hand. "I can't remember. But I do remember how that case affected you. And you want to work with cases like that all the time?"

"It's a chance of promotion."

"No," Olaf said flatly, folding his arms across his chest.

"No?" Paul's voice rose. He sounded incredulous.

"No. You can't take that job."

Paul stabbed a finger at him. "*You* don't get to decide."

"I'm your fiancé."

"Did you discuss your career change with me?"

Dammit, Olaf should have thought of that. "Touché."

"You know I wanted to make Chief Inspector by the time I'm forty," Paul said.

Paul was fiercely ambitious, and he put in the work to get where he wanted to go. It was one of the things Olaf had always admired about him. Olaf had never wanted to rise through the ranks. He had enjoyed being a detective, but he'd never had any desire to become the boss. Too much paperwork and ass-licking. The only ass Olaf wanted to lick was Paul's.

"What are you thinking about?" Paul asked.

"Why?"

"You got a wicked gleam in your eye. You're thinking about sex, aren't you? We're in the middle of an argument and you're thinking about fucking me into the mattress."

Olaf snorted. Paul knew him far too well. "Yeah."

"Take me to bed. I need your fuzzy arse next to mine."

The tension between them wasn't gone. The argument was unresolved. But they could go to bed angry and then he wouldn't see Paul for weeks, or they could make love now and let their bodies do the talking.

Olaf entangled his fingers with Paul's. "Yeah, let's go to bed."

Sometimes Olaf missed his huge apartment in Kelder. Everything in the UK was so *small*. But he'd bought the largest bed he could fit into the bedroom which meant he could throw Paul onto the bed from the doorway and grin at Paul's loud squeak as he hit the mattress.

Paul sprawled like a starfish on the unmade bed. "Bastard!" he muttered breathlessly. His scowl was adorable.

"You should be used to it by now," Olaf pointed out. "Strip."

Paul hurried to obey, tearing off his T-shirt and jeans. His hard cock slapped against his belly as he wriggled out of his briefs and socks.

Olaf waited until he was naked and then undressed himself. Some men made getting undressed part of the foreplay. Olaf just cared about getting his body over Paul's smooth skin. The years hadn't made him less fuzzy. And Paul loved rubbing his body over Olaf's. Olaf had made him come more than once from sliding his body against Paul's.

After eight years, Paul's lean body still made Olaf's mouth dry. At six foot two, Paul wasn't a small man, and the years had broadened his shoulders, but he still had an athletic build, which was a miracle considering he never did any exercise and lived on junk food when he wasn't with Olaf.

Before his last piece of clothing hit the floor, Olaf had stretched out over Paul's body and found Paul's mouth with his own, tasting the spices from their dinner. Paul gave a long, happy moan into Olaf's mouth, and wrapped his arms and legs around Olaf's body, holding Olaf so close he could barely breathe. That was okay. Breathing was a secondary consideration. All Olaf wanted was to kiss Paul until he was lost in his lover's arms.

Paul ran his hands down Olaf's back to cup his ass, repeating the motion restlessly as Olaf kissed him. He was hard and leaking pre-come already, the fluid aiding the slick movements of their bodies together.

Olaf finally pulled away from the addictiveness of Paul's mouth and slid down to suck the head of Paul's cock into his mouth, then up to the root. Paul moaned and clutched at Olaf's short hair. Olaf had let it grow out of the military-style buzzcut over the years, but it was only just long enough for Paul to clutch onto.

"Fuck!" Paul breathed as Olaf pulled slowly back until he just had the head in his mouth. "I can't keep this...I need..."

Olaf pulled off with a pop, to order, "You don't come until I say."

Paul tried to glower at him, but he was too deep in pleasure, his eyes glazed and his mouth lax.

Olaf sank back down on Paul's cock, sucking hard and hearing Paul groan. He pulled off, not wanting Paul to come yet. He reached over to the shelf that served as a nightstand, no room for the real thing, and grabbed the lube. Paul didn't need much prep. Olaf had taken him against the wall by the front door earlier in the day. But Olaf teased Paul's hole until he wriggled and begged Olaf to, "Shove your big fat dick in me before I make you."

How could Olaf resist an invitation like that?

He put Paul's legs over his shoulders and kissed Paul's hole with the tip of his dick.

Paul stared at him, his expression strained. "Please."

Olaf pushed in slowly, giving Paul a chance to breathe. Little prep didn't mean hurting his man. He pushed in until he was root to tip in Paul's body. "You feel so good."

Paul sighed and wrapped his hands around Olaf's body. "Each time feels like the first. Like I never want to let you go."

Olaf pulled Paul's ass closer to him, the change in position making Paul gasp. "I feel the same way. No matter what we do, Paul, you're mine."

Paul gave him a strained smile. "You mean that? You promise?"

Olaf hated that his cocky, confident man sounded so unsure. "I promise. You and me only."

He pushed in hard, and Paul gasped. Then he held onto Paul's thighs and fucked him, his gaze locked on Paul's the whole time. He knew his boy, knew the second Paul's screaming need to come overwhelmed him, and he nodded.

"You can come now."

Paul tried to speak, but his body's focus was solely on emptying his balls over his belly, a spray reaching his chest.

Olaf thrust hard into him and gave up trying to hold back, filling Paul's channel with his come. He pushed in once, twice more, until his thigh muscles wobbled and he pulled out gently, eliciting another wide-eyed gasp from Paul.

Five minutes later they lay, limbs entangled, still sweaty and messy, but Olaf didn't give a shit. He wanted to spend the rest of the night like this, and if they were glued together in the morning that was fine too.

"Smug bastard," Paul muttered.

Olaf furrowed his brow. "Huh?"

"Making me come on command."

Olaf smirked. "Just like a—"

"Say the word and I'll make you sleep in the spare room."

Olaf kissed Paul's sweaty forehead. "As if I would."

He grinned as Paul growled. The other bedroom was full of Olaf's gym equipment. Like

Paul would make him sleep there.

Chapter 4

Monday
"I've got to go, babe."

Olaf grumbled as Paul whispered in his ear, and snuggled down. It was too early to wake up.

"You have to let me go." Paul sounded resigned and amused.

"Don' wanna," Olaf muttered.

"I know, but the guv will kill me if I'm late for work again."

Olaf sighed and let go of his warm Paul pillow.

"Love you." Paul pressed a kiss to Olaf's temple. "I'll call you on my break. Don't forget you're going to see Charley later today."

It took a moment for Olaf to remember who Charley was. Oh yeah, his first case as a PI. He should get up and prepare. "What time is it?"

"Half four."

Olaf groaned and buried himself further under the duvet. Four thirty was way too early to get up.

"Call you later," Paul said.

"Wait."

Olaf disentangled himself from the covers and stood, pulling Paul into his arms for a slow kiss that left them both gasping when he pulled back.

"Wow," Paul murmured. "You managed to do

that without opening your eyes. How did you know where I was standing?"

"I have skills," Olaf assured him. Also there was only one space in the room where Paul could stand to get dressed.

"You certainly do." Paul patted his cheek. "Go back to sleep. Your alarm is set for eight."

Olaf pressed a kiss into Paul's palm. "You're an angel."

"Yeah, no. That's not what everyone else tells me. Gotta go."

Olaf grinned as he snuggled under the duvet again. His boy was right. Paul was definitely not an angel. But he was Olaf's.

Olaf flung out a hand to quell the obnoxious noise, missed, and the alarm clock hit the wall with a crack. The loud ringing ended on a pathetic whimper. He opened one eye and looked at the wall. Dammit, he'd gouged out another chunk of plaster. He'd have to repair the damage before his landlord saw it. Nick was fussy like that.

He flopped onto his back and stared up at the ceiling. Time to get up. He picked up his phone and checked to see if he had gotten a message from Paul. There was one.

"Did you break your phone?"

There was a reason Paul bought him alarm clocks. He'd not been happy the first time a half-asleep Olaf had flung his phone across the room and cracked the screen.

Olaf tapped a reply. *"No. Hole in wall from alarm clock."*

The response was instantaneous. *"Nick's gonna kill you."*

"He'll never know."

"Keep telling yourself that, Skippy."

After eight years, Olaf still wasn't sure who Skippy was.

He rolled out of bed, eyed the alarm clock in dislike and headed for the kitchen. His planner was on the kitchen counter. He made a note to buy a new alarm clock.

An hour later, Olaf was washed, dressed in a soft grey sweater and grey dress pants. He thought he ought to make an effort as this was a professional call. Drinking his third cup of coffee, he scanned a list of questions to ask Charley and Daniel. The only problem was, he wasn't sure what questions he needed to ask yet. But he'd been a detective for years. He could wing this. Olaf checked the clock, pleased to see he just had time for a walk on the beach to clear his head before he visited Cam's parents.

The wind off Freshwater Bay was brisk enough to raise the hairs on Olaf's arms. He sucked in a lungful of salty air. It didn't matter how long he lived here, he still marvelled in the fact he lived by the sea. He'd lived near Lake Michigan all his life, except when he was in the Marines, but this was different somehow.

He grinned as he saw a familiar face jogging towards him.

"It's a bit late for you, isn't it?" he greeted Logan Brent, his landlord's husband, and Olaf's occasional jogging partner.

"Nick was working so I worked all night. Forgot about the time," Logan confessed. He pushed his thick hair back from his face, taking out the band and tying it back again. He still looked like a Californian surfer, rather than a respected therapist. "I heard you had your first case. Slacking already?"

Olaf was not surprised the gossip had gotten this far. Nothing was secret on the island. "I'm going to see Cam's parents."

"Good idea," Logan agreed. "Listen, Nick says I ought to keep my nose out of this case." Which of course meant he was going to do the exact opposite. "But Nick told me some of the details. If you need someone to offload to, call me. This isn't an easy case."

Olaf was touched. Logan had walked away from his old life and started again on the Isle of Wight after the abusive husband of a patient had tried to kill him in a jealous rage. He'd not only left behind his home and business, but also his parents. One bourbon-fuelled night when both their partners were away, Logan had told him why. Too many secrets were spilled to be discussed in the light of day, but if anyone could understand the mindset of Bobby Sargent, it was Logan Brent.

"I will. Thanks." He grimaced. "I've already been warned off by the local cops."

"I'm not surprised. No one wants to think the worst of their colleagues."

Olaf looked at the time on his phone. "I've got

to go. Are you free for a run tomorrow?"

Logan almost nodded, then hesitated. "Can we make it the day after? Liam's coming tomorrow."

"Of course. Seven?" Olaf waved as Logan loped away.

Olaf headed to his car. He had a feeling he'd be talking to Logan professionally in the near future.

The red painted door flung open, and Charley greeted him with a delighted, "Olaf!" She reached out to give him a hug.

Cam's mom was maybe around fifty, although Olaf was useless at judging ages. She looked like Cam, with long dark hair tied up in a messy bun, the ends already escaping its confines. Olaf had only met Charley and Daniel at weddings and funerals. Both seemed to occur with monotonous regularity in their group. But he liked them both, especially as Charley always pressed a dish of something amazing into his hands.

"Come on in," Charley said. "Brunch is ready."

And this was why he'd only had a small breakfast. Although he'd declined lunch, he knew Charley would feed him somehow. It was one of the joys of his life that his friends and, by extension, their parents, took pity on him as a 'single' man and invited him to dinner. Or any meal.

Daniel looked up as he followed Charley into the large kitchen at the back of the house. "Olaf. Good to see you." He stood, and they shook hands.

"And you, sir," Olaf said.

Daniel shuddered. "Daniel please. Not sir or Mr

Gillard. That just makes me old."

"We are old," Charley said cheerfully.

Olaf kept his mouth shut. He was probably nearer their age than Cam's.

"Sit down." Charley pointed to the chair opposite her husband. "Dan's been waiting impatiently for you to turn up so he could eat."

Daniel nodded in agreement. "She wouldn't let me start without you."

"She's the cat's mother, and Olaf is our guest," Charley said tartly as she went to the stove.

"You don't have work today, sir—Daniel?" Olaf asked.

"Charley asked me to take the morning off when she got your call. I knew the Sargent family too. You know the history?" Daniel's expression was bleak.

"Some of it. His brother has asked me to find him." Olaf didn't add the dead or alive part.

Charley put a huge plate of food in front of him. "We'll eat, then you can ask questions."

Olaf looked at eggs, bacon, sausages and anything that could fit on the plate. He'd learned by now it was called a Full English. He didn't care what it was called. It was delicious. "I'm glad Paul suggested I talk to you."

Bad move. He caught the knowing look Charley shot Daniel. He waited.

"How is Paul?" Charley asked.

"He's fine. Gone back for another set of shifts. I probably won't see him for a few weeks."

Charley gave him a pitying look. Olaf focused on eating a sausage.

"It must be hard for you," she murmured.

"It's hard on both of us."

"I never understood why you didn't marry and move in with him."

"Have you seen the size of Paul's apartment?" he quipped. "It's tiny."

"You like the island, don't you, son?" Daniel said.

Olaf gritted his teeth at the 'son', but he nodded. "I do. I've loved it since Paul first brought me here for Liam and Sam's wedding. I don't really like London," he confessed.

"The island has its own charm," Daniel agreed.

Charley rolled her eyes, but she said, "I didn't think you guys would make it work, but you did. But how much longer is Paul going to wait for you to club him over the head and drag him back to his man cave?"

Olaf blinked at her. "I'm sorry?"

"Charley has this thing about cavemen," Daniel explained. "She believes men should show their feelings for their loved ones."

Olaf gave Daniel a dubious look. He couldn't imagine Daniel dragging Charley anywhere.

Daniel's lips twitched as if he read Olaf's thoughts. "I had my moments in my younger days."

"Danny got all jealous when he saw me going out with Martin Bryson. Next thing I know, Dan proposes and I'm pregnant with Cam." Charley sounded very smug about it.

"I don't think there's much chance of Paul getting pregnant," Olaf assured her.

Daniel made an odd noise, not quite a cough, more like...

"Did you just crow?" Olaf asked incredulously.

Daniel smirked and held his hand out to Charley. "You owe me a tenner."

Olaf turned to Charley who went crimson. "You bet on us?"

"She bets on everything," Daniel assured him. "It was a long time ago."

Olaf looked between them and then it was his turn to go bright red as light dawned. "Oh!"

Charley sighed. "I'm sorry, Olaf. It was a stupid joke you were never meant to know about." She scowled at her husband who had the grace to look embarrassed.

Olaf shook his head. "I guess I gave you the answer."

"You have to understand, we've known Paul for a very long time, and you are the only person who's stuck around. The only one he gave up—"

"I understand," Olaf said hastily. He knew his boy came with a reputation.

Charley laid her small hand on his. "That makes you very special. I'm glad Rose had a chance to meet you before she passed."

"I'm glad too." Olaf had not enjoyed the relationship Liam had with the matriarch of the Owenses, but he'd met her and gained her approval for his relationship with her grandson. She probably wouldn't be too happy with the way they'd dragged it out though.

They finished eating and Charley made coffee for them all before she would allow 'business' talk.

Then they both gave him expectant looks. Olaf felt as if he were a rookie detective on his first case. He pulled out his notepad, took a deep breath and started.

"As I said, Keith Sargent has asked me to look into his brother's disappearance."

"Now his old man has died," Daniel said.

Olaf made a non-committal noise. "Paul suggested I talk to you as you know the family."

Charley nodded. "Daniel knows them better than me. I remember Bobby was always getting into trouble. But the girls loved him. No one knew he was gay then."

Olaf noticed Daniel twitch. "Sir?"

Daniel scowled a little, but he said, "I knew he was gay. I was in the same class as him. He wasn't as discreet as he thought he was."

Olaf kept his expression bland. He had been another Bobby Sargent, keeping his secret hidden, always afraid he was about to give himself away, gaze too long at another boy.

Then he caught Charley's and Daniel's expressions. They knew. Of course they knew. Cameron had been lucky to have them as parents.

"So some of you knew he was gay, but what about his family? Did they know?"

Daniel shook his head. "Bobby's dad was an arsehole and free with his fists. Bobby and Keith were always coming in with black eyes. And before you ask, no one did a thing. He was a copper, and they were as thick as thieves. None of them would arrest him for disciplining his wife and kids. This was the eighties, remember. Have you ever watched *The Sweeney* or *Life on Mars?*"

Olaf shook his head.

"Well, it was the dark ages as far as the police were concerned."

Charley made a disgusted noise in the back of his throat. "At least they've changed now."

Olaf thought about his conversation with Biggsy. Maybe. Maybe not. "So what happened when Bobby disappeared?"

Daniel hesitated. "You have to understand the age of consent was twenty-one back then. It didn't change until 1994."

"And he was...?"

"Sixteen." Daniel grimaced at Olaf's wince. "He was caught by his father with a man five years older than him. It was a mess, Olaf. You have no idea."

"I can imagine," Olaf murmured.

"His dad insisted on bringing charges against the other man. Bobby was furious. He was making threats against his father, and he didn't care who heard them."

Olaf realised that his initial picture of Bobby Sargent as a shy, effeminate boy was completely wrong. Bobby could take care of himself. "He was violent like his father?"

Daniel looked horrified. "No. God, no. He wasn't like him at all."

"But you said—"

"Bobby was cocky and overconfident, and maybe a bit of an arsehole at times. But he wasn't a bully. He hated them and refused to let them cow him. He was always standing up for the underdog."

Olaf nodded as he made notes. The more he heard about Bobby, the more he sounded like Paul. "So what happened?"

Daniel sighed and Charley topped off their cups, maybe to give her husband time to collect his thoughts. "I don't know exactly what happened, but I heard there was a huge fight at their home. A neighbour called the police. You can imagine how that went down and what the cops did."

"Nothing," Olaf said flatly.

"The next day, Sargent had a black eye, but Bobby was gone. And no one's seen him since."

"What was the official story?"

"Bobby ran away in the night after beating up his father. A man three times his size." Daniel made a disgusted noise.

"And the unofficial story?"

"No one said it out loud."

"I understand." Olaf was starting to realise just how much power this man had wielded, that thirty-five years later people were still afraid to talk about it.

"They said Sargent killed him and took him out to sea and dumped his body. They had a small dinghy. Nothing fancy. But the rumour was, Sargent had been seen in the middle of the night with a rolled-up old rug, heading for the bay."

"Who started the rumour?"

Daniel shrugged. "No idea. I was a kid, remember. But nothing came of it."

Olaf sat back in his seat and tapped the notepad

with his pen. "What happened to the man who was caught with Bobby?"

"I think the charges were dropped," Daniel said. "Bobby was gone, and I don't think the police wanted that investigated closely."

"Do you remember his name?"

"No. But he didn't stay on the island. It was 'suggested' he left pretty damned quickly before Sargent got hold of him."

It was a shame, but Olaf had something to go on. "Thanks, Daniel. You've helped a lot."

"Bobby was my friend. I'd forgotten about him all these years. I was never friendly with Keith. I felt sorry for the kid. People avoided him after that. No one wanted to take the risk of being friends with Sargent's son."

Olaf's heart ached for young Keith. He'd lost his brother, he had an abusive father, and he was shunned by the community. No wonder Keith was angry. Olaf drained his coffee, before saying, "I ought to go. You've given me a lot to think about."

"My dad was friends with Sargent," Daniel said. "Of course, he had no idea what he was like until it all came out. If you want to talk to him, I can arrange a meeting."

"We'll do it here. You don't want Maureen here," Charley said.

Daniel grimaced. "My mum. She's...um..."

"A pain in the arse," Charley said bluntly. "Norman's a sweetheart, but Maureen is a cow."

Olaf stared wide-eyed between them. "Maureen is your mother-in-law?"

"She is, unfortunately." Charley grinned at him.

"You don't have to look so worried. Maureen has a reputation. I always counted Helen, that's Daniel's gran, as my mother-in-law. We all adored her, sharp tongue and all."

"That was Cam's great-gran? I think I met her once or twice."

"She was one of a kind," Daniel agreed. He looked at the clock. "I ought to get to work."

"Thanks for helping me," Olaf said, standing as Daniel did and shaking his hand.

"You're welcome. I'd like to know what happened to my friend."

Olaf kissed Charley on the cheek and left them to return to his new office. He had a lot to think about and he wanted to make more comprehensive notes before it slithered out of his mind. He really wished Paul were here, so he had someone to bounce thoughts off. After eight years they were remarkably similar in the way they approached police work. Pillow talk had developed a whole new meaning.

When he arrived back at the office, he checked his phone.

"I love you."

Olaf smiled at the screen. His boy didn't send many messages like this. He must be really missing Olaf.

He tapped out a response. *"I love you too. Wish you were here."*

"Me too."

He would drive up to see Paul at the weekend. What was the point of being self-employed if it couldn't include cuddle time with his guy?

Chapter 5

Tuesday

There was no message from Paul when Olaf woke up. He was disappointed. Paul always left him a good morning greeting, usually lewd, and sometimes accompanied by a body part. On rare occasions he was too busy to message but would contact him later. Olaf sent Paul a quick text saying he hoped to talk to him after his meeting. No body part though. Years of being in the closet had left him with a fear of someone else picking up the message.

Olaf would go to the office later. First, he needed to talk to the old copper who'd been friends with Robert Sargent. He had John Parkin's address, but the old man spent his mornings in a pub in Ryde. Olaf decided to confront him there.

He stood in the doorway of the pub, seeking his quarry. The barroom was dark and at this time of day, not full of tourists. There were several men who fitted the description he'd been given. Older guys hunched over tabloid newspapers. It was only just ten in the morning, but they all had a half-drunk pint of beer in front of them. He admired their fortitude. Maybe he'd get past the falling asleep at lunchtime stage once he retired.

"John Parkin?" he said, raising his voice.

A grim-faced elderly man wearing a dark green jacket looked up from his crossword. "Who wants to know?"

Olaf walked over to him and held out his hand. Parkin didn't take it. Olaf let his hand fall. Parkin was going to make him work for this. Olaf wasn't surprised. Parkin looked as if his life was etched in the lines of his face, and it had been a grim one.

"I'm Olaf Skandik."

"The Yank cop."

He wasn't surprised that Parkin knew who he was. "Yes. May I join you?"

"It's a free country."

Olaf stayed where he was and finally, Parkin rolled his eyes.

"Get me a pint, and I'll listen to what you have to say."

Olaf refrained from pointing out he was more interested in what Parkin had to say. "Sure. What do you want?"

Parkin named one of the beers on tap.

Olaf went to the bar and gave the order to the bartender, a cute blonde with a long ponytail. He added an Americano for himself.

"I'm surprised he's talking to you." She placed the beer in front of him. "He ignores everyone else."

"I'm the lucky one," he said with just a trace of irony.

Her lips twitched, and she wished him good luck. He took the drinks back to the table.

Parkin waved impatiently at him. "Well, sit

down. I've been expecting you."

"Biggsy or Sam Owens?"

"Danny Gillard."

Olaf should have expected that. Cameron's dad wouldn't have wanted the old man to be blindsided. Still Olaf wished he hadn't. He preferred to get the element of surprise when interviewing suspects.

"You know why I'm here."

"You're on a fool's errand," Parkin said bluntly.

"You think tracking Bobby Sargent's whereabouts is a waste of time?"

"It's been thirty-five years. Why rake up the past?"

"Keith wants to know what happened to his brother. Wouldn't you if your brother had gone missing?"

Parkin shrugged. "I'd be happy if my brother had stayed missing. Never could abide him."

Olaf smiled but he waited for Parkin to get to the point.

"Bobby was always a troublemaker. I'm not surprised he ran away. He got caught..." Parkin's top lip curled giving no doubt of his feelings about that incident. "...and rather than face his father like a man, he vanished like the coward he always was."

"He was a kid," Olaf pointed out, keeping his tone as mild as he could, even as he felt righteous anger on behalf of the betrayed sixteen-year-old boy from many years before.

"He was man enough to stick his dick where it shouldn't be," Parkin retorted.

Olaf picked up his cup and took a long swallow of coffee rather than spill the angry words that were on the tip of his tongue. The drink was hot and welcome as it burned through him.

"Tell me about Robert Sargent senior."

"Why?" Parkin demanded.

"You were his friend. Everyone I've spoken to so far has been Bobby's age. You knew him."

Olaf's phone buzzed. A message. He didn't look at it, keeping his attention solely focused on the old man.

"He was a good copper. On the beat his entire life. Didn't want to be a guvnor. We were very similar. We liked being on the front line."

Olaf got it. He wasn't much different to Parkin. He'd never wanted to be management, unlike Paul. "He was liked by the people on his beat?"

Parkin hesitated. "He was respected."

"Did he ever have a problem with anyone?"

Parkin gave him a scornful look. "He was a policeman."

Olaf guessed that answered the question.

"I can't be expected to remember every toerag from forty years ago."

"Anyone who stands out?"

Parkin huffed loudly. "I thought you were here about Bobby Sargent."

"I've talked to other people about Bobby. I wanted to talk to you about Robert."

His phone buzzed again. He was going to catch it from Paul for ignoring him for this long.

"He was a good man," Parkin insisted.

"But he abused his wife and kids."

Parkin frowned, obviously not liking the line Olaf was taking. "He kept discipline in his own house."

"He hit them," Olaf pressed.

"Once or twice," Parkin said reluctantly.

Olaf snorted. "And when the police were called, he never faced any charges."

"Would you do that to one of your mates?"

"If I knew a co-worker was beating his wife and kids? Yes, I would. Then? I don't know. I wasn't there. You were." He let the last words hang in the air.

Parkin took a moment, then he flushed angrily at the implication. "He was a friend."

Olaf let it slide. It was a different era. Parkin knew he was in the wrong. There was no point beating him with it, and Olaf hadn't intended to antagonise the man.

"You haven't asked me if I thought Robert killed his boy."

"No, I haven't."

"Why not?"

"It's obvious you don't think he did."

Parkin grunted. "For what it's worth, Robert loved his sons. He was quick to anger, and we all knew it—"

Olaf kept the sneer off his face with an effort. Quick to anger. An interesting way of describing a violent man.

"—but he adored them. He thought Bobby was going to take after him in the police force. The kid always talked about being a policeman. It broke his heart when Bobby vanished." Parkin gave him a fierce stare. "He knew what people thought of him. What young Keith thought of him. But he was a proud man, and he wouldn't back down. You know he hired a private detective to find Bobby?"

At last! Olaf almost cheered. How many times had he been given the most useful information as a by the way? "Do you remember the name of the private detective?"

"I do. Stuart Reynolds. Not that it would do you much good. He was in his sixties when he worked for Robert. The guy's been dead twenty years."

It was disappointing but to be expected. "Did Reynolds live on the island?"

"Yes, in Freshwater. Near the bay. I can't remember the road."

Olaf wrote down a note. He lived in Freshwater but, more to the point, so did Logan and Nick, and Nick knew everyone. Reynolds might still have family there. "Thanks for the information."

Parkin sat back in his seat and looked at Olaf. "You know Bobby might not want to be found."

Olaf nodded. "I know. Just before I go, can you remember the name of the boy caught with Bobby? The one who was arrested?"

Parkin wrinkled his nose. "No."

"After Bobby's disappearance you let him go."

Parkin shrugged. "Nothing to hold him on. Robert was too upset to press charges."

Olaf nodded. "Thanks, Mr Parkin."

"You're with the youngest Owens boy."

"I am." Olaf waited for a snide remark.

"He's a damn good copper."

Olaf smiled at him. "He is."

"Pity he's a—"

"Goodbye, Mr Parkin."

Olaf turned on his heel. He didn't need to hear the end of that sentence.

Just outside the pub, his phone buzzed again. He pulled it out to see five missed calls and seven messages. What the hell? Before he could do anything, the screen lit up with Paul's work number at Darrow police station.

Olaf connected the call. "Paul?"

"Olaf. At last. It's Andy Bunch."

Fear clutched its icy hand around Olaf's heart. "Andy. What's happened? Where's Paul?"

"I'm sorry, mate. He's in the A&E at St Hughes."

Chapter 6

Tuesday

For a moment, Olaf thought the world had stopped. He couldn't hear the sounds of the cars passing him, the people talking in excited voices. Then he was shoved from behind and he could hear again, but too loudly, as if someone had turned the volume up extra loud.

"You're standing in the doorway," a man grumbled, then he was gone down the street and Olaf was back in the world.

"Olaf? Did you hear me?"

Olaf heard Bunch's worried voice. "Yes, I'm sorry. How...badly is he hurt?"

"He's got a skull fracture, a concussion and a broken nose, and his right arm is in plaster."

Okay. Okay. Not serious. Skull fracture! *Paul is fine. Deep breaths, Skandik. Focus.*

"What happened?" he asked.

"A bloke got lively in the custody suite last night. He was hammered. He took exception to Paul's pretty face."

Last night? He's been in hospital all this time and they tell me now? Then *thank God I didn't drink a pint.*

Olaf knew Bunch was trying to make him feel

better, but it really wasn't working. He'd been shot when he first met Paul. Paul had watched it on the TV in Liam's hospital room. They'd only just met each other at that point, but Paul had once confessed he still had nightmares about it. Now Olaf knew how he felt.

"Anyway, Paul wasn't going to tell you, but you're his emergency contact, and he'll need to be picked up from the hospital if they discharge him."

Of course Paul wasn't going to tell him. Olaf clenched his jaw. He was going to kill his lover slowly and painfully, concussion or not. "I'm on the next ferry. When's he going to be released? If it's soon, I can get his mum to pick him up."

"That's great. And tell him not to think of coming back to work. The chief super has banned him from the building for the next two weeks."

Olaf barked out a laugh. "I'll bring him down here."

"That's a relief," Bunch admitted. "You know he's a nightmare when he's bored."

Olaf had an excellent way of occupying Paul, but he didn't need to discuss that with his colleague. "Leave it with me, Andy. I've got to go. I've got a ferry to catch."

"Thanks, Olaf. And don't worry when you see him. He's banged up but he'll be fine and as annoying as ever."

Olaf would reserve judgement until he saw his boy for himself. As for annoying, that was a given.

As soon as he disconnected the call from Bunch, he called Paul's mom. He strode towards his car as he waited for her to answer. He heard a click, then he held the phone away from his ear as seventies rock was blasted into his ear, only to be turned off abruptly.

"Hi, sorry about that," Mattie said breathlessly.

"Mattie, it's Olaf."

"Olaf, sweetheart. I was going to call you at the weekend about your new job. How are you?"

"Mattie, Paul's in St Hughes."

"Is he okay?" Fear infused her voice and Olaf hurried to reassure her.

"According to Andy Bunch, a skull fracture but not serious, a broken arm, concussion, and bruising on his face. I'm heading to my car, and I'll get the first ferry over, but could you talk to the hospital and maybe collect him if they want to release him? He was taken in last night, but I've only just found out."

Mattie let out an impressive stream of curse words. Olaf grinned. Paul was going to be in trouble with Mattie as well as him.

"Jim can pick him up. You said St Hughes?" Mattie asked.

It was the closest one to Darrow Road police station where Paul worked.

"Yes."

"We're on our way. Are you driving up?"

"I'm in Ryde. I'll head for the ferry now. Just let me know if I'm driving to you or the hospital. And when you see him, tell him I'm gonna kill him."

"With pleasure."

"And will you tell Sam and the others?"

"I can do that."

Then she was gone, and Olaf got in his car. It wouldn't take long to get to the ferry terminal. He just hoped it wasn't busy and he wouldn't have to wait too long for a space.

He pulled into the terminal to see lines of cars waiting for the ferry. He was unlikely to get on the next one.

He opened his window to see a man he knew from The Blue Lagoon beaming at him.

"Olaf, I didn't expect to see you leaving the island. How's the new case going?"

Olaf forced a smile. "Fine, thanks, Chris. I need to get a ticket. Paul's been injured at work."

The smile faded from the man's face. "Okay, mate, you go and park down there and we'll get that sorted for you."

Olaf parked where he was told and headed into the ticket office. It was empty bar a woman behind the counter. She smiled at him as he approached. "Are you Olaf?"

"Yes."

"Let's get your registration number. As soon as we're done here, drive down and wait at the bottom. You're on the next ferry."

He forced a smile, grateful that Chris had obviously called through to expedite matters. "Thank you and thank Chris for me."

Olaf hoped he hadn't kicked someone off the ferry, but most of him didn't care. He just wanted to get to Paul.

"I will," she said. "Off you go. They're already loading."

Olaf jogged back to the car and drove down

towards the car ferry. He was waved onward as soon as he got there. Fifteen minutes later he sat at a table with a coffee in front of him and called Mattie.

"I'm on the ferry."

"That was quick," she exclaimed.

"One of the Blue Lagoon customers was at the gate."

"Good. I've phoned the hospital and spoken to Paul. He's okay. Grumpy as all hell, but okay. He told me to tell you not to come, but I told him to shut up."

"He doesn't want me?" Olaf sucked in a breath. That was like a punch to the gut.

"He's dazed and confused and embarrassed. Ignore everything that comes out of his mouth for the next twenty-four hours. His skull has a hairline fracture, but he'll be fine. They're discharging him in a couple of hours. Jim is already on his way. You come here and I'll make you dinner. You can stay here for the night. I don't think Paul's going to want to go anywhere."

Olaf would have preferred to be on his own with Paul, but he realised Mattie was as freaked out as he was and wanted her son close to her. "I'll swing by his place and collect clothes for both of us."

"Good idea. Drive safely, Olaf. Don't look at your phone on the way up."

Olaf blinked, offended by the idea that Mattie thought him that irresponsible. But then she said, "He needs you here in one piece."

"I'll be there," Olaf promised, his voice gentle.

"See you soon."

Mattie sounded choked up as she disconnected the call and Olaf realised how close to tears she was. Police work had its dangers and Olaf had been on the frontline too. But it was much worse when it was your loved one hurt.

Olaf sighed and pulled out his notebook. He still had forty minutes of the journey to go. He could think about his interview with Parkin. He scanned the notes, adding in thoughts as they came to him. Something the man had said bothered him, but he couldn't put his finger on what it was. He'd gotten the answers he was expecting from Parkin. The guy was a friend of Sargent senior after all. But there was something...

Gah! If he'd a chance to think about it right after the interview maybe he'd have remembered, but now his mind was too caught up with Paul to focus. Still, he spent the rest of the journey making notes and suggestions for what to do when he returned to the island, hopefully tomorrow. The private detective, Stuart Reynolds, was an unexpected discovery. It was too much to hope that his family had kept his notes, but someone might be alive who remembered the case.

He put away the notebook as the Tannoy squawked out a message for them to return to their cars. Olaf's stomach rumbled. He hadn't thought about food. The café was still open, so he picked up a sandwich and crisps for the journey home. In his head he still called the crisps potato chips, but Paul always mocked him when he did. Liam once told him that on his first trip to the Isle of Wight he'd wished people spoke proper English because he needed a translator. Olaf had laughed with him, both of them having that feeling many times.

He sat in the car, munching on the food as he waited to disembark. His phone buzzed and he looked at the screen.

"Wish you were here."

Olaf smiled and assured his lover he would be in his arms soon.

Paul's flat was a disaster zone. Paul usually kept it tidy but when he worked nights he didn't care. He slept, and he worked on repeat. Sometimes he ate. Usually when Olaf nagged. Paul cleaned up his flat just before Olaf arrived. This time Olaf got to see the mess in all its glory. He briefly contemplated tidying, but he wanted to see Paul more than a clean kitchen.

He filled a backpack with a change of clothes for them both and toiletries. Then he headed to Paul's parents. The schools were disgorging their pupils as he drove, adding more time to the journey. By the time he arrived he had a pounding headache and tense muscles from shouting at the oblivious kids spilling into the roads in front of him and the parents taking up the space in their SUVs, which had never done anything more than brief trips to the supermarkets and schools.

Olaf grabbed the backpack and headed for the door. He raised his hand to bang on the door, only for it to open without warning.

Jim smiled at him, but Olaf could see the lines of tension around his eyes and mouth. "Hi, Olaf. He's in the lounge. I'm warning you. He's grumpy."

Olaf felt some of the tension leave his body. Grumpy was normal. Grumpy he could deal with.

Jim stood back so Olaf could walk down the hall and into the lounge. Paul was in one corner of the sofa, a huge scowl on his face. At least Olaf thought it was a scowl. It was hard to tell through the bruising. Olaf's heart did a flip-flip as he looked at the swollen eyes and nose, and split lips. His right arm was in plaster from his fingers to his elbow. Paul had taken a real battering. If the man who'd hurt Paul had been within reach, Olaf wasn't sure he could have controlled his anger.

Paul looked up as Olaf entered the room. "What the hell are you doing here? You're supposed to be working. You've got a job to do."

"Shut up," Olaf muttered, dropping the bag, and striding over to Paul. "Just shut up."

Then he was next to Paul and hauling him—albeit gently—into his arms. He felt resistance, then Paul curled into him, and Olaf swore he heard a sob. Paul smelled rank, sweat and blood overlaid with hospital scents, but Olaf didn't care. He would take that for having Paul in his arms.

They stayed like that for a long while, Olaf muttering in Paul's ear. If challenged afterwards, Olaf wouldn't have been able to repeat what he said, but it boiled down to 'I'm here, I love you, I'm here'. Paul, who wasn't that keen on over-the-top displays of affection, stayed enfolded in Olaf's arms and didn't move. Olaf realised Paul had fallen asleep. He was content to stay where he was, grateful Jim and Mattie had given them a few moments to be alone. He needed it to control his own feelings, anger and fear bubbling so close to the surface.

But eventually Jim poked his head around the door. "Do you want a coffee, Olaf?"

Olaf smiled at him. "Please, Jim." He stayed where he was though. He wasn't going to let Paul go for a second.

Mattie came in with a cup which she placed on the table next to him. Then she bent to kiss him on the cheek. "He couldn't relax until you were here."

Olaf kissed the top of Paul's head. "I was just the same. If I don't get a ticket after the speed I drove up here, I'll be surprised."

She sat on the edge of the other sofa and fixed her gaze on him. He felt like a butterfly pinned under a microscope.

"You two can't go on like this."

Olaf didn't pretend not to understand. He and Mattie had had too many similar conversations. "I know."

"He's hurting."

"I know."

"You're hurting."

Olaf didn't think she needed a third 'I know'. That wasn't the answer she wanted. Mattie hated Paul being in the police force. It had been a source of contention for years. Paul had admitted he joined the police mainly to annoy his mother, except it turned out he was a damned fine police officer. What Mattie wanted was for Olaf to sling Paul over his shoulder and carry him back to the Isle of Wight to live happily ever after. What was it about mothers and cavemen?

"He's told you about the promotion?" she snapped.

Olaf pressed his lips together. "He has."

"You can't tell me you approve."

He glared at her. "Of course I don't." He kept his voice low, not wanting to wake Paul.

"Then *do* something."

"Like what, Mattie? I've told him how I feel about it. But I can't stand in the way of his promotion. It has to be his choice."

"Rubbish. He's crying out for you to take charge."

Olaf gave her a cool look. "Just because I top him in bed doesn't mean I control the rest of his life." That side of their life was no secret to anyone, thanks to Paul's blabbermouth.

She had the grace to blush at the implication, but Mattie, being Mattie, forged on ahead. "That job will kill him."

"I know. I've told him that. I remember what he was like with the Fryer case."

"He was a wreck," she said bluntly. "Drink your coffee."

He startled, having forgotten about it. Paul muttered and grumbled, then settled back to sleep. Olaf waited for Paul to settle then he picked up his cup.

"He's got to see it for himself, Mattie. If I force

the issue, and he comes to the island, he could resent me for the rest of his life. You know how ambitious he is."

"I know how ambitious he was," she agreed. "But I think he's starting to realise that ambition isn't everything."

Olaf gave her a dubious look. "He's never said that to me."

Mattie glanced at her son. "I think he's afraid of letting go of what's motivated him for so long."

"This is not really the time for any decisions. We're all freaked out by what's just happened."

Olaf was trying to be calm and rational, even though he wanted to do exactly what Mattie said. Pick up Paul and put him into his car, drive to the island and never let him back. He was more than freaked. He was a seething mass of fear and anger. Not to put too fine a point on it.

Mattie gave him a knowing look. Olaf kept his expression as calm as he could. One thing he had learned over the years, his kind-of-mother-in-law had a scarily accurate bullshit detector.

"Leave the boy alone, Mattie," Jim said as he came into the room. "He's just got here, and he doesn't need you yelling at him."

Mattie huffed and sat back in the sofa. "I'm sorry, Olaf. You're right. I am freaked about what happened. This is every parent's nightmare. We're just lucky it wasn't worse."

Olaf inclined his head. He'd had this same discussion with his own mom when he was deployed overseas in the Marines and when he joined the sheriff's department. "What about the skull fracture?"

"They aren't worried about that. It's minor. But as he's got a concussion he's got to rest."

Olaf breathed a sigh of relief. He'd been more worried about the skull fracture than anything else. "I'll make sure he does that."

Paul opened his eyes and blinked up at him, his brown eyes sleepy. "Hey. When did you get here?"

"Don't you remember me arriving?" Olaf asked, ready to drive him to hospital there and then.

"Uh…oh yeah. You told me to shut up. Twice."

Olaf dialled back the panic. Paul could remember that and scowl at him, so he was fine.

"Are you here to take me home?" Paul asked.

"Do you want to go to the flat?" Olaf hoped not. He really didn't like staying in Paul's flat for any length of time, but he couldn't leave Paul there to manage by himself.

"No." Paul yawned, and closed his eyes again. "I want to go to our home."

It had always been Paul's flat and Olaf's place. Never *their* home. Olaf blinked back the sudden tears. This was Paul with his barriers down, saying what he really wanted. Olaf couldn't hope for too much but, yes, he'd take his lover back to the island right now if he could.

He looked up to see Mattie and Jim staring at them. He raised an eyebrow. "Yes?"

"Nothing. Nothing at all," Mattie said in an innocent tone. "You'll stay the night?"

Olaf's answer was cut off by Paul sitting bolt upright, saying, "I'm gonna barf."

Mattie grabbed the bowl on the table and shoved it towards Paul just in time. Olaf grimaced and looked over Paul's head as he retched noisily.

"I don't think we'll be going anywhere until he stops vomiting."

"I think you're right," Mattie agreed.

Chapter 7

Wednesday

Paul took a deep breath, his face ashen under the bruising. Olaf hunkered down in front of him and put his hands on Paul's knees, to stare into his bloodshot eyes. He winced just to look at the mess of Paul's pretty face.

"Are you sure you're well enough to travel? We could stay here another night."

"Not in that bed I'm not," Paul muttered. "I'm not spending another night without you."

Olaf wholeheartedly agreed. He'd slept on the floor next to Paul's single bed, and he hadn't gotten much sleep, constantly waking up to check Paul was okay. That had disturbed Paul, and they'd both woken up tired and grumpy.

"Do you want to go to your flat?"

Paul shook his head and then groaned and held his head. "I wish I hadn't done that."

"Idiot," Olaf said fondly and kissed Paul's forehead. "Let's go home. We'll take bowls and bags."

He stood and left Paul where he was. It didn't take long to book a ferry for the early afternoon. Then he packed the backpack and threw it in the car. He came into the house, pausing in the hall when he heard Mattie talking to Paul.

"Make sure you rest."

"Yes, Mum."

"And take time to think about what you want to do."

"Not now, Mum, please." Paul sounded desperate.

Olaf was about to intervene when Mattie spoke again.

"He's a wonderful man, Paul. Is your ambition more important than Olaf?"

"It's not that easy."

Olaf leaned against the wall and closed his eyes. He tried not to feel hurt. It wasn't like he didn't know Paul put his work before their relationship. Maybe once upon a time that had been true for him too. He could have moved to London rather than insisting he lived on the island.

"Isn't it?" Mattie demanded. "You two have spent the past eight years dancing around each other. You're not twenty something anymore, son. It's time to settle down."

"And make baby Owens for you?" Paul asked sarcastically.

"I'm quite sure Olaf would insist they are baby Skandiks." Mattie didn't sound fazed. "But I've got enough grandchildren. I'm more concerned about my youngest boy and his lovely partner."

Olaf was touched that Mattie included him. And relieved that she didn't want the two of them to produce grandchildren. They'd decided a long time ago that they didn't want kids. Paul swore he never wanted to grow up, and Olaf had never cared about reproducing.

"We're fine, Mum."

And now there was a hint of a whine in Paul's voice. Olaf decided to intervene before his high-maintenance lover got more upset. He needed to stay calm until he was over his concussion.

Jim came out of the kitchen with a cardboard box and saw him lurking. They smirked at each other. "Can you give this to Sam? It's just old photos. I forgot to take them down last time we were there."

"Sure."

Olaf took the box and put it in the back of the car. Then he returned to collect his fiancé before he lost the will to live.

Paul looked up in relief as Olaf walked in. "I thought you'd run away."

"Not this time, lover. Let's go home."

He wrapped his arm around Paul and helped him to his feet, ignoring Paul's hissed "I'm not that helpless."

It didn't escape Olaf's attention that Paul leaned into him. When Olaf looked at Mattie, he saw her roll her eyes. He grinned at her, and she returned it.

Paul took a deep breath. "Okay, I'm feeling better now. Let's go, big guy. I want to see my island and my bed."

"I could carry you."

"Do it and die," Paul said flatly.

Olaf kept an arm around him and led him to the front door. "You lean against me."

Paul let his mum hug him and dad pat him on

the shoulder. Then Olaf got him into the car and helped him with the seatbelt, ignoring Paul's grumbles. It wasn't like Paul was going to manage with the cast.

Olaf slid into the car and turned to him. "Wish I'd carried you now?"

Paul leaned back and closed his eyes. "Just take me home."

Olaf grinned and started the car.

"I hate you," Paul muttered.

"I know."

"You're laughing at me."

Olaf laid a hand on Paul's thigh. "With you. I'm laughing with you because I love you."

Paul sighed. "You know just the right thing to say."

Olaf jumped at the knock on the window. Mattie stood there with a bowl. Olaf opened the window and she handed it to him.

"You'll need this."

"Okay, but he's not been sick today."

Paul took the bowl from him. "Thanks, Mum."

Olaf wondered if he was missing something, but he thanked her and finally they drove away.

Killing his fiancé was against the law. Olaf kept reminding himself that. The journey had seemed to last an eternity, between Paul grumbling that he couldn't go back to work and retching miserably into a bowl. Olaf was on the point of leaving the A3 and driving to the nearest hospital when Paul admitted that he got travel sickness, especially when he was feeling unwell.

"How come I don't know this?" Olaf demanded.

"Because it doesn't happen often. More when I was a kid. And normally when I feel ill, I stay in bed. I'll be fine. I just need to get into bed and stay there."

Paul's face was almost as white as his T-shirt. Olaf looked at him dubiously, but Paul was an adult. He really hoped Paul was telling him the truth.

They hid in a corner for the ferry crossing. Fortunately, the sound of Paul's suffering seemed to keep anyone from bothering them.

And finally, they were home. Olaf steered Paul into the bedroom.

"Do you want to get undressed?"

"No. I just want to sleep."

Paul slumped onto the bed. Olaf knelt at his feet and pulled off his shoes. Then he helped Paul under the duvet.

"How's your arm?" Olaf asked.

When Paul hesitated, he said, "An honest answer."

"It hurts like a bitch," Paul confessed.

"Painkillers, then sleep."

He ignored Paul's grumbles as he left the bedroom, returning a moment later with a glass of water and medication. He placed them on the shelf, then looked at Paul who had his eyes shut.

"Wakey, wakey. Take the pills," Olaf ordered. "You'll sleep better."

Paul scowled but he allowed Olaf to ease him into a sitting position. He took the medication and sighed with relief as he lay down, with a pillow to support his arm.

"Go to sleep, sweetheart."

Paul mumbled something. Olaf couldn't hear it but when he studied Paul, he realized he was already asleep. Olaf brushed his lips and told him he would never let Paul go. He was sure Paul smiled in his sleep.

As Olaf made himself coffee, he called the one person he knew would be waiting.

"Where are you? Are you home yet? I'm on my way."

"Shut up, Sam. Hi, Liam," Olaf said easily, knowing Sam would put him on speaker. "Yes. We're back. No, don't come here yet. Paul's asleep and I don't want him disturbed. He's worn out."

"So are you," Liam said.

"I am. I'm going to work briefly, then nap."

"I'll bring you dinner tonight," Sam said.

Olaf rolled his eyes but there was no point protesting. Sam would fret until he'd seen his brother. "Okay, but later. Much later."

"I'll make sure he doesn't come around until after seven," Liam said.

"But—" Sam protested.

"I'm driving." Liam could be quite firm when he chose to be. "Get some sleep, Olaf."

"Yes, sir."

Olaf disconnected the call before Sam had a chance to protest. He was shattered, but he knew he wouldn't have a chance to relax until he'd taken a look at the Sargent case. He'd received no calls which wasn't unexpected. The business wasn't officially open yet and he'd sent a message to his client to tell him he was following a new lead, but he would be on the mainland for a couple of days because Paul had been hurt. He received a polite reply hoping Paul was all right.

He typed Stuart Reynolds into Google just to see what turned up. He blinked when the first hit was Stuart Reynolds, private investigators, but now it was based in Portsmouth. He clicked on the website. It may have been a one-man band in the eighties, but now it was a company with many investigators.

Who ran the show?

He clicked through the website. David Reynolds. Son? Grandson? Olaf couldn't put an age on the man.

Still, there was a good chance that they'd have Stuart's records somewhere. But would they talk to him?

Only one way to find out. He tapped the number into his phone.

"Stuart Reynolds, private investigators. Becca speaking. How may I help you?"

"My name is Olaf Skandik. S-K-A-N-D-I-K. Is Mr Reynolds available?"

"He's busy at the moment," she said smoothly. "We have other investigators available. Could you tell me what services you're looking for?"

"Actually, I want to talk to him about Stuart Reynolds and one of his old cases. Are there any other family members free?"

"No, just Mr Reynolds. I'm afraid I can't—"

Olaf cut her off. "Look, take my number and pass the message onto Mr Reynolds. Tell him I'd appreciate it if he got back to me. It's about the Bobby Sargent case."

"Okay. But Mr Reynolds is away at the moment. It won't be for a few days."

"That's fine."

Olaf gave Becca his number and disconnected the call. It was disappointing but not unexpected. He only hoped David was sufficiently intrigued to call him back.

The first yawn caught him by surprise. The second one cracked his jaw. He needed a nap. Olaf wandered into the bedroom and looked at Paul who was sleeping peacefully. He needed to be next to Paul for at least a few hours. He stripped down to his boxers and eased around Paul, careful not to jog his arms. Paul murmured, and he froze, but Paul settled down again.

Olaf laid a hand on Paul's thigh, and Paul wriggled back to press against him. Olaf closed his eyes. His boy was back in his bed where he should be.

"All right, all right, I'm coming," Olaf yelled.

He'd been woken from a sound sleep, and he was ready to kill whoever was thumping hard enough to break through the damned doorway.

He flung the door open, unsurprised to see Sam, Liam behind him holding a covered casserole dish. Sam scowled at him, then his expression changed as he raked his gaze over Olaf's almost naked body.

"Sorry we...interrupted you."

"Fuck off," Olaf muttered. "I thought you

weren't coming around until after seven."

"It's nearly eight," Liam pointed out. "Have you been asleep this whole time?"

They'd been asleep for nearly five hours. It felt like five minutes.

Olaf yawned. "We didn't get much sleep last night. I'll get my robe."

"Where's Paul?" Sam asked.

"Asleep upstairs."

"No, I'm not."

Olaf turned to see Paul yawning as he walked down the stairs.

"Who the hell was making the noise?" Paul asked.

"He was." Olaf pointed at Sam, expecting a quick retort, and then saw the stricken look on his face as he stared at his brother.

"Paul. What the hell happened?" Sam said.

"Bloke kicked off as he was being booked in. I went in to help and got in the way of his fists." Paul touched his mouth ruefully. "He could sure pack a punch."

Suddenly Sam's face crumpled, and he stepped forwards to wrap his arms around his brother. Paul patted his back awkwardly with his uninjured hand.

"Okay, okay, you sap. Let me go."

Sam stepped back and wiped his face with his hand. Liam drew him into his embrace and offered him a tissue. Once again Olaf was reminded of the bond between the two brothers. They were the youngest of the Owens boys and Sam could be as protective of his younger brother as he was of Liam. Paul was the same, he just refused to admit it.

Paul looked at Olaf. "Much as I like you standing there naked, lover boy, maybe you should find some clothes?"

"You really are fuzzy," Sam said.

"Yes, he is," Paul purred.

"I can buy you a razor."

"Touch one hair and die," Paul said flatly.

Olaf snorted and patted Paul's butt as he went to find something to wear. He returned a few minutes later in his sweats and hoodie, feeling relaxed for the first time since he'd gotten the news from Bunch.

Paul was curled up on the sofa, a cushion supporting his arm. Sam sat next to him. They were deep in conversation. Liam was nowhere to be seen but Olaf could hear clinking in the kitchen. He left the two brothers to talk and went to find Liam.

"That smells good," he said as he walked into the kitchen.

Liam grinned at him. "Chicken casserole. A recipe from home."

"Home?"

"It was my mother's recipe. Well, as close as I can get to it seeing as I can't ask her." Liam focused his attention on the dish. "Logan asked me what good things I remembered about my childhood, and this was one of them."

Olaf nodded. "You're still seeing him?"

He knew the answer already, but he wanted to encourage him to talk. Liam's wry smile told him he saw right through that ploy.

"I am. It helps, you know, and thanks to the settlement I can see Logan on an ongoing basis." Liam pulled a face. "Although if I'd known how many years of hard work it was going to be, I'd never have let Jeff drag me to that first visit."

Olaf knew that if that first visit hadn't happened, there was a good chance Liam wouldn't be here now. The Owenses could never thank Jeff enough for realising Liam was in crisis, and Logan for bringing Liam back from the brink.

"Still." Liam huffed out a breath. "The result is chicken casserole. The kids on my course love it. And Jeff's curry."

Olaf rolled his eyes. "You're feeding your course mates?"

"They told me it was a thing. By the time I realised I'd been had, it was too late."

And Liam loved every second of mothering the kids. Who was Olaf to judge? Particularly if he got to taste the results.

"How's the case going?" Liam asked.

"It's like trying to unravel yarn," Olaf admitted. "I keep pulling at the end only to discover another knot."

"You'll be good at that."

Olaf was warmed by Liam's ready praise. "I ought to go back to the office tomorrow. Pretend I'm actually running a business."

"But you don't want to leave Paul?" Liam asked knowingly.

"I'm worried he'll run back to work."

"I'm not at uni for the rest of the week. I've got

assignments to write, and I could do with somewhere quiet to work. I could man your office if you want."

Olaf gave him a doubtful look. "One, will your guard dog let you out of his sight and two, wouldn't you rather be with Paul?"

Liam raised his hand, but the brothers were still talking. "One," Liam said in a low voice. "Sam has to work in Portsmouth for the week, and I don't want to be sitting in the house waiting for him to come home. Two, I'll never get anything written if I babysit Paul. And three, Wig has promised me coffee on the house for helping him out, and I'm determined to collect."

"I think he owes you a lot more than a coffee," Olaf observed.

"He does. But even extracting coffee from him is a miracle. He goes on about Nibs being tight, but Wig has gotten a firm hand on the purse-strings."

"Is the dinner ready yet?" Sam asked as he wandered into the kitchen. "Paul is getting whiney."

They all grinned at the disgruntled, "Fuck you!" from the main room.

Olaf noted that Sam seemed calmer now he'd seen his brother.

He left Liam and Sam to serve the casserole and went into the lounge to find Paul poking at his fingers peeking out from the bandages.

"What are you doing?" he asked.

"My fingers are swollen."

"That's not surprising. Your eyes and mouth

are swollen too."

"Next time that guy is going down."

Olaf sat next to him and took Paul's injured hand gently in his. "Next time you get out of his way." He didn't bother to say there wouldn't be a next time. There was always a drunk guy in custody.

Paul huffed, but he leaned closer to Olaf. "Thanks for bringing me home."

Olaf kissed the tips of his swollen fingers. "Always."

"I should have called you sooner."

"You should." Olaf let the hint of a growl in his voice, knowing the effect it had on Paul. Sure enough, he got a shiver. "Why didn't you call me?"

Paul refused to meet his gaze. "I wanted to prove I could manage without you."

Olaf captured Paul's chin in his and turned his bruised face to meet him. "And what did it prove?"

"I was an idiot. I needed you there."

"Yes, you did. Don't do it again."

Paul rested his cheek against Olaf's palm. "I won't. Mum gave me hell for it. Then Dad did too."

"Jim?" Olaf asked doubtfully.

"His exact words were 'I thought you were growing up, son'."

"Ouch."

"I'm lying on the hospital bed, bruised and battered. My nose had just started bleeding again. He's holding a tissue to my nose and telling me off at the same time. You can guess how that made me feel."

"Poor baby," Olaf crooned.

"Hungry baby. Is Liam raising that chicken from an egg?"

"Quit bitching," Liam said as he came into the room with two plates.

Paul poked his tongue out, and Liam grinned.

The casserole was delicious, and Olaf praised Liam more than once between shovelling in huge mouthfuls.

Sam stared at him wide-eyed. "Jesus, big guy. No one's going to steal your plate."

"Missed lunch," Olaf pointed out.

"There's more in the pot," Liam said.

Olaf noted Paul was poking at his food. "Aren't you hungry?"

"It hurts to eat," Paul confessed.

"I've got just the thing," Liam said, and vanished back into the kitchen.

Five minutes later he returned with a bowl which he placed on a tray in front of Paul.

"You made me chicken soup?" Paul asked.

Liam nodded. "I blended some of the casserole into soup. I brought it just in case."

Olaf took Paul's plate of chicken casserole and started eating. He saw everyone staring at him.

"Waste not, want not," he said.

Chapter 8

Thursday

The next day, Olaf thought he should get back to his case, but after an hour, he had to admit he was stymied. Until Reynolds got back to him, he couldn't pursue that lead and he didn't have another. Paul was asleep in their bed, as he'd been most of the morning, and Liam was in the office for him. By the time lunchtime arrived, Olaf was bored and frustrated. He made himself a sandwich and sat down at the table to work.

He reread his notes. In a few days he'd managed to gain an understanding of the Sargent family. He'd met many like them in the past. Parkin had been honest. Yes, Robert Sargent used his fists. But he'd loved his kid enough to employ a private detective. Maybe Keith Sargent knew something about that. He messaged Keith and five minutes later his phone rang.

"Mr Sargent."

"Keith."

"Keith," Olaf said. "Do you remember if your father ever spoke about Stuart Reynolds?"

There was a pause. "The private detectives in Portsmouth?"

"You know them?"

"I spoke to them first before I came to you, but they didn't seem that enthusiastic. I get the feeling they're interested in bigger fish than me."

Olaf pinched the bridge of his nose. He could feel a headache brewing. "According to John Parkin, your father employed the original Stuart Reynolds to look for your brother."

Another pause. "I didn't know that. I remember him because he lived near us."

"I've put a call into their office, but the current Mr Reynolds is away. He's going to call me back. Have you looked through your father's papers?"

"Not all of them."

"It might be worth seeing if your father kept anything from Stuart Reynolds. A report or something."

"I'll do that. Thanks for everything you've done so far."

"I haven't really gotten anywhere."

"You know a lot more than I did. Why didn't Dad tell me he'd hired a PI to find Bobby?"

"Maybe he didn't want to raise your hopes if Reynolds couldn't find him?" Olaf suggested.

"But at least I would have known that he hadn't given up on Bobby. Or that he hadn't killed him," Keith admitted finally.

"Or he did that to throw people off the scent," Olaf warned. His years as a detective had shown him just how devious people could be. And Robert Sargent had been a police officer. He would know what the cops would be looking for.

Keith sighed. "My dad could be that manipulative," he admitted.

"I'll report back to you as soon as I've spoken to Mr Reynolds," Olaf said. "In the meantime, I'm going to hunt down more of Bobby's friends."

"I've been thinking about that too. Bobby didn't have many friends at school, but I'll send you a list of people I know. Most have moved off the island now, but one or two are still here."

"What about gay friends?"

"I was a kid. He kept me away from that. Dad would have gone mental if Bobby had introduced me to any poofs. No offence," he added hastily.

"None taken," Olaf murmured. He'd been called worse, especially once his co-workers in the sheriff's office found out why he was leaving.

"I can remember one or two guys who kept coming around. They were older than Bobby. Dad didn't like it, but Bobby didn't care. He was a shit to Dad. They were always at each other's throats."

Olaf felt extremely sorry for the younger Keith, caught in the middle of the feud.

"It was peaceful when Bobby left," Keith admitted. "And Dad was easier to live with. It was only later I began to wonder what had happened to Bobby. Whether Dad had killed him. Bobby's disappearance seemed to eat him up, you know?"

"So you wondered if he was guilty?"

"Yes. I felt so bad at first thinking the worst of him, but he became more and more unbearable to live with."

"He could have just been feeling guilty about giving Bobby a hard time. I'll track down more of Bobby's old friends. Daniel Gillard will probably help me."

"Cameron used to babysit my kids. He's a good lad."

"He is," Olaf agreed. "He's one of my best friends."

"If Bobby had stayed, maybe he would have ended up with a circle of friends like you." Keith sounded wistful. "How is Paul?"

"He's bruised and beaten, with a broken arm, and a concussion."

"Was it a fa—queer bashing?"

Olaf winced at his terminology, but he appreciated Keith's clumsy attempt to be considerate. "No. A prisoner kicked off in the custody suite. Paul got in the way of his fists."

"Dad used to come home with bruises. Particularly after a Friday night."

Olaf heard a noise and looked up to a naked Paul shuffling into the room, his eyes half-closed. "I've got to go, Mr Sargent—Keith. Call me if you find out anything about Stuart Reynolds."

He disconnected the call, left his phone on the table, stood and held his arms out to Paul who shuffled into them and rested his face in the crook of Olaf's neck.

"How are you feeling?"

Paul groaned in his ear.

"That good, huh?"

"Tea?"

Olaf still hadn't been able to break Paul's habit of drinking tea. "Coming right up."

He held Paul for a moment longer, then guided him to the couch before wrapping him in a soft throw. Paul lay back and closed his eyes again.

Paul would probably be asleep before Olaf made the drinks, still, he'd take that chance.

He returned a few minutes later to find Paul snoring gently. Olaf thought about going back to work, but he decided to take a break for a few moments and snuggle up to his man.

"Where's my tea?" Paul grumbled as Olaf sat down.

"I thought you were asleep."

"Not sleeping," Paul muttered.

Olaf grinned at him. "Liar. You have to open your eyes if you want your cup."

"I can drink with my eyes closed. I've had years of experience."

But he sat up, cracked open one eye, and made grabby hands at the cup. Olaf handed it over and watched Paul take a long swallow and sigh with relief.

"Do you need painkillers?"

"No. Just more tea."

Olaf gave him a sceptical look, which was totally wasted on Paul as he had closed his eyes again. Olaf sighed and kissed Paul's cheek.

"I'll fetch you another cup of tea."

"Ta babe." Paul leaned against the couch.

Olaf watched him for a moment. He knew Paul would feel better soon. It was only just over forty-eight hours since he'd been hurt. But it didn't stop Olaf worrying about his lover.

"Quit staring at me and make me a cup of tea."

"Bossy bastard," Olaf said fondly and went into the kitchen. If Paul was well enough to be rude to him, he must be feeling better.

Despite his protests Paul fell asleep before he drank the tea. Olaf left it on the table to get cold. He wasn't going near it. Paul slept in his arms for the rest of the afternoon. Olaf let Paul snort and snuffle against his chest while he read a book on surveillance on his Kindle.

It was almost six before Paul raised his head. "Guess I missed the tea, huh?"

Olaf kissed the top of his head. "You did. Want me to make you another one?"

"No. Just stay where you are so I can rest on you." Paul sighed and lay back on Olaf. "When am I going to stop sleeping?"

"Your brain took a battering. It needs to recover."

"I should be back at work," Paul said. "I can do desk duty."

Olaf wrapped his arms around Paul. "No fucking way, Paul. You're not going anywhere for two weeks."

"But—"

"I mean it. You're going to stay here. I'll handcuff you to the bed if necessary."

Paul snorted. "Kinky. But let's remember you're the one who gets handcuffed."

Olaf flushed because, yes, he was, and he loved it. But he would wrestle Paul into submission to force him to rest. "Not this time. You take one step out of here and I'm cuffing you to the bed."

"I don't think I've got the strength to fight with you," Paul admitted.

Olaf knew what an admission that was. Paul never backed down. He kissed Paul's temple.

"You'll feel better soon, I promise. I know how I felt after the shooting."

Paul rolled so he was on his back, looking up at Olaf. "You don't mind me being here? I could go home."

Olaf waggled his fingers as if he was cuffing someone.

"You can go off people, you know," Paul said sourly, but he didn't make any attempt to move from Olaf's lap.

Olaf pushed Paul's hair back from his face. The bruising was fully out now, and his face was a mess of purple and black swelling.

"Not so pretty now," Paul murmured.

"You will always be beautiful to me," Olaf said. He caressed Paul's cheek, careful not to press against the bruising.

Paul raised his uninjured arm and cupped Olaf's jaw. "You're all bristly."

Olaf rubbed his bristles against the palm of Paul's hand. "I haven't bothered shaving since you left."

"I like you with a scruff."

Olaf had always shaved as a cop, but maybe now he'd let go a while. He smiled at Paul. "You're getting a beard yourself."

"You know I never get a decent beard, and I'm not growing a goatee."

Olaf grimaced. "For which I'm very thankful."

Paul wriggled, and Olaf had to clamp his arms around Paul to prevent him ending up on the floor.

"What are you doing?" Olaf asked.

"Trying to get up," Paul said, obviously frustrated. "I'm desperate for a wazz."

"Careful! Let me help." Olaf eased Paul into a sitting position, then helped him to his feet.

As Paul staggered off to the bathroom, Olaf went into the kitchen needing coffee and something to eat. The book had held his interest more than he thought it would and he hadn't bothered to get a drink for himself.

"I feel like shite," Paul admitted on his return.

Olaf had returned to the couch. "Why don't you go back to bed?"

"I'm sick of sleeping," Paul grumbled. "But I feel like if I sit down, I'm going to fall asleep again. We could watch a film."

"You're not supposed to watch TV or look at screens," Olaf said.

"Great. What am I supposed to do?"

Olaf held out his arms. "How about cuddle with me, and I'll tell you about this book I've just read on surveillance."

"Kill me now," Paul muttered, but he went willingly into Olaf's embrace.

"Never scare me like that again," Olaf muttered into his hair.

"No promises," Paul murmured. "I'm Paul Owens, remember?"

Olaf kissed his hair. "How could I forget."

Friday

By the time the next day arrived, Olaf was climbing the walls. He needed to get out of the house. Unfortunately, Paul had slept all morning and woken up with the mood from hell. It was Olaf's fault. He'd foolishly made the suggestion that Paul talk to Logan.

"I don't want Logan to pick my brain apart," Paul snapped.

"Even if it will make you feel better?"

"I got beaten up by a drunk bloke. That's all. There's nothing to psychoanalyse."

Olaf wanted to push it, but Paul looked so defeated as he pushed the remains of his lunch around his plate that he didn't have the heart.

"Fancy a trip out?" he suggested.

"To the pub?" Paul sounded excited for the first time since his return to the island.

"If we could do one thing first, I'll take you for a drink."

"Done. What do you need to do?"

Olaf gave him a wicked grin. "You should really have asked that first."

"I should have done. I didn't think about that. My brain isn't working." He sighed and rested his chin on his good hand. "What are we doing?"

"Searching Sargent's house."

Paul's eyes lit up. "Are we looking for dead bodies?"

"Yes, Paul," Olaf said dryly. "We're totally searching for dead bodies."

"Wait, I've got a concussion, but I can search a house?"

"Technically, you're not there. You can sit on the couch and look pretty as I want to keep an eye on you. Also we'll have Keith's permission to search his property. We're not hunting for criminal activity."

"I thought we were looking for a dead body."

Olaf counted to ten.

Paul smirked at him. "Which language are you counting in this time?"

"Welsh."

One of the advantages of being on his own so much was time to learn multiple languages.

"Welsh." Paul looked impressed. "Way to go, babe. And how are you doing?"

"I can count to twenty. Not much more than that," Olaf admitted.

"How many languages can you count to ten in now?"

"Not nearly enough to handle you," Olaf assured him.

Paul looked very smug about that.

Olaf called Keith Sargent, but he didn't receive an answer, either by phone or text. If Keith was at work, he could be driving. Olaf decided to take a chance. They both needed to get out of the house before they killed each other.

"Come on, let's go for a drive," he said to Paul and picked up his keys.

"Corpse-hunting and beer. What more could a boy ask for?" Paul pretended to flutter his eyelashes.

"Glad I can show my boy a good time," Owen said.

"Someone likes gardening," Paul observed.

Keith Sargent's front garden—Paul had trained

him out of saying yard—was full of lush, blooming, pink and red flowers.

"Do you want to stay in the car?" Olaf asked.

"No, I'll come with you. I could do with a walk." Paul grimaced. "Everything is aching."

"I can drive you home if you want," Olaf offered.

"No way," Paul said. "You promised me a beer."

Olaf watched him groan as he got out of the car. The chances of Paul making it to the pub were slim.

He followed Paul up the driveway to the front door, squeezing past a shiny new caravan. "Keith followed up on his promise."

"Huh?" Paul looked confused.

"His wife wanted a new caravan. We could have a caravan vacation." He chuckled at Paul's horrified expression. "Not something that appeals to you?"

"How can I phrase this?" Paul pretended to think. "No."

"But sweetheart—"

"Continue this and we're through," Paul said flatly.

Olaf's lips twitched as he pressed the doorbell. His fiancé had some very fixed ideas about things.

The front door opened, and a woman with long red hair and thick-rimmed glasses studied them suspiciously. "Can I help you?"

"Mrs Sargent?"

"Yes," she said, clearly still wary. "I'm not religious and I don't buy anything from the doorstep."

Olaf was taken aback. Did they look like salesmen or missionaries? "My name is Olaf Skandik. I'm a private investigator. This is my partner, Paul Owens."

"Owens?" She raised her eyebrows, obviously more interested in Paul's family than who Olaf was. "One of Rose's grandkids?"

"Yes, Jim and Mattie's youngest," Paul said in the long-suffering tone of one who'd answered this question many times before.

"Ah. I thought I'd seen you around. What can I do for you? Aren't you a police officer?"

"Paul's helping me," Olaf said, hoping to capture her attention. "Is Keith at home?"

She shook her head, and Olaf noticed she wore dangly earrings which bobbed as her head moved. "Sorry, he's at work today. Are you the private detective?"

"I am. I wondered if we could take a look around his father's house?"

"I'd say yes but I don't have a key. We gave the spare to the estate agent, and Keith's got the other."

"That's a shame," Olaf said. "Could you give me the address? We can at least look around the area."

She still looked suspicious, then Paul said. "I'm a cop, and Olaf was a detective until a couple of weeks ago. We won't take or break anything."

She let out a breath. "I'm sorry. I know I'm being ridiculous. My name's Miriam, by the way." She shook Olaf's hand and took Paul's hand carefully. "What happened to you?"

"A drunk took exception to my face at work,"

he explained.

"It wasn't me," Olaf assured Miriam as she still hesitated.

She blushed. "I didn't think that."

"It's okay. It's understandable," Olaf said, "but I promise I'm not like Robert Sargent."

Miriam looked over her shoulder and then back at them. "He was a vile man," she said in a low voice. "He nearly broke my Keith. I'm not sorry he's dead. I just wish it hadn't taken so long. That makes me sound awful, doesn't it?"

Olaf looked at her, hoping she didn't see any judgment there. "You had to live with him in your life," he said. "No one has a right to judge you for how you feel. No one."

Her smile looked relieved. "I guess you've seen some awful things as cops, haven't you?"

"We have," Paul agreed. "The worst. Don't worry about a natural reaction."

Miriam nodded. "Dad—Robert—lived a few roads from here."

Olaf offered her a notebook. "Could you write down the address?"

"Is this the house Keith grew up in?" Paul asked as she scribbled.

"It is. Dad wanted me to move in, but Keith couldn't wait to get away from the place. We tried to persuade Dad to move into something smaller, but he said that was his home and he refused to move out." Miriam offered the notebook to Olaf.

"He was attached to his home," Olaf suggested.

"Maybe he was worried they were going to find Bobby's body," she snapped.

Olaf took a step back, and she realised what she'd said.

"Dammit. Sorry. It's just been a long day. Keith is…he's not doing well. Whatever you find, understand it's going to be hard on all of us. We've lived with this our entire marriage."

Olaf glanced at Paul and then at her. "Tell me honestly, what do you expect us to find, Miriam?"

She folded her arms and glowered at him behind the thick-rimmed glasses. "Nothing. I don't expect you to find anything. And that will be the hardest of all for Keith, because he'll have to live with it for the rest of his life."

That was honest, if not encouraging.

Paul shuffled next to him, and Olaf saw how pale he looked.

"Go back to the car," he murmured to Paul who took the keys and left without protest.

"Take him home," Miriam said. "He's exhausted and pretending that he's okay."

Olaf chafed at the order, but she was right. Searching Sargent's place could wait for another day.

"Will you tell Keith I called?"

"I will." Miriam studied him for a long moment. "Take care of Paul, Olaf. The man in your life needs to know you have his back."

"Keith is lucky to have you."

"He is," Miriam agreed. "And the kids. Don't screw up, Olaf. Or I'll be after you."

"I'm not a miracle worker," he protested.

"No, but Keith's put his faith in you. Don't let him down." Then she closed the door before he could say a word.

Olaf stared at the door for a moment then jogged back to the car. He wasn't surprised to find Paul asleep again. Guess the beer was out.

Chapter 9

Saturday

Olaf woke feeling like he'd been drugged. He smacked his mouth a couple of times and rolled over to find Paul staring at him. Paul had obviously been reading. He wore glasses and an open book was in his lap. He refused to use an ereader even though Olaf pointed out the benefits of being able to increase the font. Paul did not like being made to feel old. But still, it was odd to know Paul had been staring at him in his sleep.

"You know that's creepy, right?" Olaf pointed out.

Paul shrugged. "I like staring at you, fuzzball. Deal with it."

"Fuzzball? Are you serious?" Now Olaf was offended. He had body hair, but he wasn't a goddamn bear like Nibs. He wouldn't mind being a bear. Instead he had this short blond fuzz all over him. Men had liked the feel of it. Paul *loved* it. He'd gotten off more than once just rubbing over Olaf. But fuzzball was too much.

He opened his mouth to complain again, but then he caught Paul's expression. It was clear that something was up with his boy.

Olaf wriggled closer to Paul. "What's wrong?"

"Nothing."

"Bollocks. Talk to me. You look as if I kicked your puppy. If we had a puppy. Which we don't." Olaf found himself mumbling with a finger over his mouth.

"Jesus, Olaf, take a breath."

Olaf kissed the finger. "Then talk to me."

"I don't want to go back," Paul admitted.

"You don't want to go home or back to work?"

"You don't think this is my home?" Paul sounded hurt.

Olaf sat up, sitting back against the headboard so that he could haul Paul into his arms. "This is your home, sweetheart. Here, in my arms. But you can live wherever you wish."

Paul sniffed, and Olaf realised he was close to tears. "Smooth talker."

Olaf stroked his hair, soft now Olaf had washed it. "You want to live here with me?"

"I do. But I can't."

Another sob.

Any other time Olaf would have pushed the matter, but what was the point? This had to be Paul's decision. Not his. If Paul stayed on the island, he would give up the career he'd wanted for so long.

Paul's face was buried in Olaf's shoulder. "I feel so guilty."

Olaf blinked. "But why?"

"I forced you to come over here."

"You didn't force me to do anything," Olaf said. "This was my decision."

"Because I wouldn't go to Kelder."

"You didn't want to step into a tightly locked closet," Olaf said gently. "And I knew that. Besides, the only way we could be together with me as an openly gay man was for me to move here."

"You left your family and friends behind. And your job. You loved that job."

"I did, but I loved you more."

Paul sighed. "I gave up nothing."

"You gave up being Paul Owens. You gave up your reputation." Olaf huffed. "I should have moved to London."

"But you hate my flat," Paul almost wailed.

"I do," Olaf admitted. "But just because it's so small. We could have gotten a bigger apartment."

"You hate London."

"I love you. I could have made it work."

"But here you have the boys. Your friends."

That had been a large part of his decision to get a job on the island. He had Liam and Sam, plus all the other guys. And this was a way to get Paul down here away from work.

"I love living here," Olaf agreed. "I felt like it was home the first time I came here for Liam and Sam's wedding."

Paul sighed. "And you got to meet Gran."

"Rose was a special woman."

The matriarch of the Owens clan had been a formidable woman, but the family loved her, and were devastated by her death. Olaf was glad he'd gotten to meet her before she passed.

Paul sat up and looked around. Olaf handed him a box of tissues. Paul took one, wiped his eyes and blew his nose.

"You know I never wanted to live here," Paul admitted.

"I know."

"I liked visiting, but it wasn't exciting enough for me."

"I know that too," Olaf agreed. Paul seemed so vulnerable yet wanting to talk. Olaf didn't want to stop him. They had danced around their relationship for so long.

"All I could think when that guy was hitting me was *exciting* wasn't all it's cracked up to be."

"What are you saying?"

Paul sighed. "At the moment I have no idea. I just know we have to make changes. And I'm scared out of my brain that you'll go home to Kelder and leave me."

"I'm not going to leave you, Paul."

"You mean it? You're not going to change your mind again?" Paul's gaze was locked on his. This had obviously been worrying him.

"I'd like to go home and see my mom and dad. It's been a while. But you could come with me. We could make it a vacation."

It was a suggestion he didn't expect Paul to agree to. Paul had always been adamant that he saved his vacation for somewhere hot.

"I'd like that. If I can get the guv to agree."

"We could go on a sun, sea, and cabana boys vacation afterwards," Olaf suggested.

"Let's spend time with your parents. The cabana boys can wait."

Knowing what a sacrifice that was for Paul, Olaf decided to show him how thankful he was.

Normally he'd have rolled to his back and let Paul ride him until they were both senseless. But Paul wasn't quite ready for that.

Olaf nestled Paul in the pillows and settled between his legs. "I'm gonna blow you and you are gonna lie back and think of England."

"I'd rather think of cock," Paul grumbled.

"You can take my cock later. Now..." Olaf licked his lips. "...it's your turn."

Paul wiggled and sighed. "I'll go with that."

His cock thickened under Olaf's heated gaze.

"You haven't even touched me, and I feel like I want to come."

"Not until I'm ready," Olaf warned.

Paul raised an eyebrow. "You still think you can make me come on command."

Olaf gave him a slow, heated smile. "I know I can."

He dragged a slow finger down Paul's uncut cock from root to tip, making sure he brushed the leaking tip to make Paul shiver.

"Bastard," Paul hissed.

"Yours."

"Promise?"

Olaf had to remember that, for all his brashness, his man could be just as insecure as the rest of them. "I promise there's no one else in my life except you, and never has been since the day we met."

"You hated me."

"You were everything I was afraid to be. And I hated you for making me want more than I allowed myself."

"But you wanted to fuck me," Paul said smugly.

"I wanted to fuck you through the mattress and never let you go."

Olaf moved so he could kiss that smug look off Paul's face. When he pulled back, Paul's eyes were glassy and his mouth puffy. "Kissed is a good look on you."

"You're the only person who turns me inside out," Paul murmured.

"Good. No man—or woman—is ever going to see this look again."

Olaf tried never to forget Paul was open in his attraction. Did it bother him that Paul had fucked women too? Yes, it did, but Paul had told him from the start to get over it. Paul was his now, and that was all that mattered.

"Possessive bastard." But it was clear Paul loved every minute of his possessiveness.

Olaf slid down the bed and licked up Paul's hard shaft. He nibbled back down. Then he sucked Paul's tight sac into his mouth, rolling the orbs with his tongue. Paul whimpered and Olaf smiled.

"Suck me," Paul demanded.

Olaf kissed his sac, then he feasted around the glans until Paul writhed beneath him. He held Paul's hips, and sunk down on his cock. It didn't take long. They were both too much on the edge to last. Olaf pulled back to the tip, then sunk down, firm suction around Paul's dick.

"Fuck! Fuck!"

Paul shouted as he arched his back and came, spasms shooting down Olaf's throat. Paul had barely pulled away when Olaf raised up. He grabbed hold of the headboard and frantically tugged his cock. It took seconds and, as he reached his tumultuous climax, he remembered their Skype sessions and coming so hard his semen hit the screen, covering Paul's image. Watching the stripes coat Paul's chest and face was so much better.

Olaf walked into his office bearing gifts. He'd left Paul sleeping soundly after their lovemaking. Liam was hard at work. He had a crazy number of textbooks spread over the desk. He looked up, initially with a professional smile, then a real one as he spotted what Olaf held in his hands.

"I bring coffee," Olaf said.

"You're an angel." Liam made grabby hands for the takeout cup. "I forgot to bring milk. Where's your sidekick?"

"I brought milk too. Paul is talking with his boss about returning to work. We want to take a vacation first."

Olaf decided not to mention Paul's reservations. If he told Liam, he would tell Sam, and then the whole family would know.

"Isn't he still recovering?"

"Paul is fretting."

"Ah." Liam nodded in understanding.

Olaf decided a change of subject was in order. "Wig said you were looking tense today."

Liam rolled his eyes. "You know that I know, that's Wig code for Liam looks shite and go talk to him before Sam does his nut."

Olaf shrugged. "And that."

"I look shite because Sam's away, and I've taken the opportunity to work all night."

"I thought only kids pulled all-nighters."

"Are you saying I'm old?"

Liam's indignant look faded quickly as Olaf smirked at him. Olaf was a few months older than Liam.

"You're right though," Liam admitted ruefully. "I'm way too old to be staying up all night."

"So why are you? I thought you were doing okay in your course."

"I was. I am. But this is my final exam. I want to ace this. I'm thinking of doing the masters next year."

Olaf had a sudden flashback to the John Doe unconscious in the bed eight years before. This man had changed his life around. Liam had been to hell and back since then, but now he was a different man.

"That's wonderful news," Olaf said sincerely. "What does Sam think?"

"He loves the idea." Liam pulled a face. "He's happy I'm happy."

"He would give you the world on a silver platter if he could."

Liam sighed and stared down into the cup. "I know. I just wish I could do the same for him. He's working too hard. He needs an assistant."

"Can he afford one?" Olaf knew Sam's business had boomed, but that didn't mean to say he was able to take on staff.

"If he let me pay."

"From the compensation money?"

Liam had finally gotten a substantial payout from the sheriff's office where Olaf had worked, as it had been a member of their staff who had hit Liam in a department vehicle.

Liam nodded. "I could invest in his business."

"But he won't accept it."

"No. Sam says I should save it to help with my recovery. I deserve it. I told Sam helping him would make me happy, but he won't listen."

"Could you work for him?"

Liam wrinkled his nose and shook his head. "My head doesn't work so well since the accident."

"You're about to graduate in Philosophy. You want to do a masters," Olaf pointed out.

"Figures were never my thing. He needs someone who can do the book-keeping."

"Also working with your other half is never a good idea."

Liam gave a wry smile. "I adore Sam. My love for him kept me alive...well, you know. But doing this course has given me a new purpose in life. I don't want to give it up now. Sam needs someone who can hit the ground running, not someone who needs to be trained and is busy elsewhere."

"All good points."

"I wouldn't mind manning your office though. When I'm not in uni, and most of my work is still online. It's quiet here. My neighbours keep bringing me cake. They still feel sorry for me."

"I can't afford to pay you," Olaf pointed out.

Liam laughed. "You know I don't need your money. I just need the space. Which reminds me. You had a visitor. A man." He pulled his notebook towards him. "Tony Dobson. At a guess I'd say mid-forties. He wants to talk to you about the Sargent case. I took his number. Also you had a call from a Jace Comerford. He wants to talk to you about an assignment. He's off the island until Friday, but he's made an appointment for three pm. I said you might not be able to focus on it immediately, but he said he didn't mind."

"You're hired," Olaf said immediately, and Liam's face lit up. "Once you agree it with Sam."

"You know I'm an adult and capable of making my own decisions," Liam pointed out.

"And you know that the whole family will be involved in this business so you may as well ask them up front." Olaf hesitated, but finally he bit the bullet. "Talk to Logan about it."

Liam's scowl deepened. "You want me to talk to my husband *and* my counsellor about taking a non-job manning your office?"

"Liam, what's been my first assignment?"

"What do you mean—Oh."

Olaf saw the flinch, the moment Liam understood what Olaf was saying.

"You're trying to find a gay kid who was thrown out by his parents. Like me."

"Like you," Olaf agreed. "And I think that this won't be the only case. Gay men need private detectives too. And not just gay men."

For the first time he voiced the feeling that he would get the cases the LGBTQ+ community didn't want to bring to the usual private investigators.

Liam sat back in his seat and bit on his nail.

Olaf waited patiently, knowing Liam needed to work this through in his head.

"You think it could affect my recovery?"

"I have no idea," Olaf admitted, "but I love you, and I won't do anything that could put you back in that dark place again."

Liam's smile was sweet. "I was so lucky to find you all."

"I'd like to point out *I* was the one to find *you*."

Liam rolled his eyes at Olaf's smirk. "Yeah, yeah. Smartass. I'll talk to Sam and Logan. I think I'll be fine though. I want you to find out what happened to Bobby, but it hasn't affected me on an emotional level."

Olaf hesitated, but eventually decided to say what had been on his mind anyway. "I could look for your parents."

"No," Liam said.

"You don't want to know what's happened to them?"

"Since they threw me out, you mean?"

Olaf winced. When it was put like that...

Liam smiled at him. "I worked through all that with Logan. I made my peace with what my parents did a long time ago. I've been so lucky. I had Alex, and now Sam, Rose and Mattie and Jim. Plus everyone else and you guys. Even Tea and Kathy. I have the best family ever."

"Good." Olaf was pleased to change the subject and he wouldn't push it. Not everyone needed to rehash their past. "Now how do I convince my fiancé not to take that promotion?"

"Have you looked at Paul lately?" Liam asked.

"I look at him all the time." It was true. Olaf never took his eyes off Paul.

"I mean, really look at him." At Olaf's blank stare, Liam said, "Paul is desperate to stay here. With you," he added, obviously convinced Olaf was still floundering in the dark.

"But his career—"

"Keeps him lonely and overworked, and away from you. If he'd been offered a promotion he actually wanted, I'd have said you had a fight on your hands. But this move is a poisoned chalice. That might work in your favour."

Olaf sighed and got up to make more coffee. Liam shook his head when Olaf waved the cup at him. "If I pressure him to stay, he'll grow to resent me."

"Then don't. Just be there for him. I'm surprised he's not stuck his nose into this case."

Olaf snorted. "He's spending the day chasing down Bobby's gay friends. My boy has contacts everywhere."

Liam didn't look surprised. "Have you ever thought he could come into business with you?"

"Of course I have. But he likes the high-powered work. Would it be enough for him? And could the business support both of us?"

"All good questions." Liam closed his books. "If you're here, I'm going to meet Sam for a coffee on Ryde Pier."

"Do you still feel Alex there?"

"Sometimes," Liam admitted. "Normally when he's got something to say."

With anyone else, Olaf would have suggested

they see a doctor if they heard their dead best friend's voice in their head, but they'd all grown used to Alex's presence in Liam's life. Even Sam, who just requested Alex stay out of their bedroom. Alex had been bossy in life. It made sense he was bossy in death. It occurred to Olaf that if it hadn't been for Alex's final bequest to Liam, he wouldn't be here now.

"Olaf?"

Olaf blinked and caught Liam staring at him. "Huh?"

"Are you okay?" Liam asked.

"Sorry, I was lost in thought."

"Okay. Is it all right if I leave my books here? Sam and I have promised ourselves a date night. No working or studying."

"What are you going to do?" Olaf asked.

"Fuck each other senseless." Liam blushed but he had a twinkle in his eye.

Olaf chuckled. He should have known better than to ask. "Get out of here. I'll see you tomorrow."

Liam was halfway out the door when he turned, saying, "Thanks, Olaf."

"What for?"

"For mentioning Logan. It's a good idea. You should get Paul to see him."

"I suggested the idea. It didn't go down well."

Liam's smile was positively wicked. "Arrange an intervention like Jeff did for me. He didn't give me any choice."

Olaf had bent to grab the milk from the fridge, but he stood and gave Liam a thoughtful look.

"That's a good idea."

"Just don't tell Paul it was mine," Liam begged.

"What's it worth?" Olaf teased.

"I thought you were such a nice boy when we first met," Liam said. "Now you're blackmailing me?"

"I love an Owens brother. And Paul Owens at that. How long did you think nice was gonna last?"

Olaf grinned at Liam's laughter, topping the dark liquid off with milk as neither he nor Liam had gotten creamer, despite the fact they both grumbled every time they used milk.

He picked up the notes Liam had left on the desk. First, he tapped the meeting with Jace Comerford into his planner on his phone, then he called Tony Dobson. If the man had made an effort to visit him, it had to be important.

"Yeah?"

"Mr Dobson? It's Olaf Skandik."

"Who?" The voice sounded blank.

"You visited my office earlier?"

"Oh yeah, the private detective."

Olaf waited. When the man didn't say anything, he said, "How can I help you?"

"Sargent did it." The words seemed to tumble out in a rush.

"Did what, sir?"

"Killed Bobby. He killed Bobby."

Chapter 10

Saturday

Olaf took a deep breath. "What makes you think that, Mr Dobson?"

"Because Bobby said he was going to."

Even through the phone Olaf could hear his pain, but also fury. Suddenly the office door opened, and Paul walked in, wearing his sling this time.

Olaf held up his hand and mouthed, "Important."

Paul frowned, but he nodded and perched on the edge of the desk.

"Are you still there?" Dobson snapped.

"I am. I'm sorry, Mr Dobson," Olaf said. "You said Bobby told you his father would kill him?"

Paul turned to face him, his eyes wide, but he didn't speak.

"Bobby never stopped saying it," Dobson said. "He was convinced his dad was going to kill him. But there's something else."

"Yes?"

"My dad saw Sargent carrying something in a rug from his house the night Bobby vanished."

Olaf let out a breath. Could this be the break he'd been waiting for? "Mr Dobson, could we meet to talk more about this?"

"I'm only free this afternoon. I'm back on shift tomorrow. Listen, I don't want to talk about it in the house. My wife knew the family, and she wouldn't be happy if she knew I was talking to you."

"We could meet for coffee in the Blue Lagoon," Olaf suggested.

"Aye." Dobson didn't sound impressed. "I'll be there in half an hour."

He disconnected the call without a farewell.

Olaf let out another explosive breath and placed his phone on the desk.

"Well? Give!" Paul demanded.

"That was Tony Dobson."

Paul furrowed his brow. "Dobson. Dobson. Why do I know that name? What did he want?"

"He says Bobby told him Sargent was going to kill him," Olaf said.

"That doesn't mean he did," Paul pointed out. "Teenagers say their parents are going to kill them all the time."

"But Dobson also said his Dad saw Sargent carrying something rolled up in a rug away from the house, the night Bobby disappeared."

"Shit." Paul whistled. "So maybe Sargent did murder and dump his kid in the bay."

This was not the kind of lead Olaf wanted. "I want to talk to him, to find out whether this is true or bullshit."

"You're meeting him downstairs?"

"Yeah. In—" Olaf looked at the clock. "—twenty-five minutes."

"I'll come down with you and talk to Wig while you chat to him. I know the name, but I don't know why."

Olaf pressed a grateful kiss to the palm of Paul's uninjured hand. "I have a feeling your local knowledge will be invaluable."

Paul snorted. "I thought I was going to have to fight you on this."

"This is my first case. I need all the help I can get," Olaf admitted.

"You've found out more than I thought you would. People like talking to you."

Olaf pinked a little under his lover's praise. It was bullshit of course. He knew he intimidated people. Of the two of them, he felt Paul was the better cop. The biggest, nosiest pain in the ass, but the better cop. People spilled out their life history to Paul.

"What made you come here?" he asked, changing the subject.

"I thought we could catch up with the boys. I invited Jeff and Cameron, and Logan and Nick, for a drink. Wig and Nibs have to work so it was easier to meet here."

"Not Sam and Liam?" Olaf teased, knowing what the answer would be.

Paul shot him a sour look. "Like I could leave my big brother out."

Olaf got to his feet and pulled Paul against him. Paul gasped and his eyes closed. "I've got twenty minutes, and I want to kiss you."

"Just kissing?"

"Can you come in ten minutes to give me time

to wash up?" Olaf asked.

Paul rolled his eyes. "Of course I can."

Then Olaf looked at him and a thought occurred to him. "Can you support yourself with your arm?"

"I've got two."

"You won't be able to jack yourself off."

"You'll have to work extra hard, then, won't you? Lock the door and get on with it," Paul snarled.

Olaf took Paul at his word. He was strong enough to hold his man and God, he needed to be buried in Paul right now. He leaned over and locked the door, then he turned Paul around, placed a kiss at the nape of his neck and yanked Paul's sweats and briefs down, hearing the satisfying slap of his cock against his belly.

"Easy," Paul breathed.

Olaf studied Paul's butt, which made his mouth water as much as it had the first time he'd seen it. He slapped Paul's ass cheek, hearing the satisfying crack against his palm.

Paul looked over his shoulder and glowered at him. "Hey."

Olaf raised his eyebrow. "Yes?"

Paul grumbled, but his head went down, his ass up and ready for Olaf.

Olaf smiled. He pushed Paul's T-shirt up and trailed soft kisses down Paul's spine to the swell of his ass, feeling Paul shiver under his hands. If he'd had time, he would have rimmed Paul's hole until he was crying out, but that would have to wait.

"Lube?" he asked.

"Desk drawer."

"You put lube in the drawer?" Olaf asked faintly as he reached into the drawer. Dear God, had Liam found it?

"I'm always prepared." Paul stretched and sighed.

"Thank you, sweetheart."

Olaf flipped open the cap and squeezed the lube onto his fingertips. He rimmed Paul's hole with his fingertips, loving Paul's gasp as he pressed in two fingers, pumping slowly in and out, careful not to jog him.

"We're on a deadline here, babe," Paul reminded him.

"I know," he said easily.

Olaf could bring him off in five minutes. He knew Paul's body like the back of his hand. He unzipped his pants with one hand and continued fucking Paul with the fingers of the other.

"Timing," Paul warned, but his voice was tight.

Olaf grinned. Paul was ready for him. He pulled his fingers out and pushed his cock in, in one smooth motion. Paul cursed underneath him. Olaf was always impressed by the language Paul could bring to their lovemaking. He could make any word sound dirty.

"Three minutes," Paul gasped.

"Brace yourself," Olaf warned as he hauled Paul against him, and changed the angle.

"Fuck!"

Olaf hesitated. "You okay? Need me to slow down?"

"Not if you want to keep your knackers," Paul

snapped.

Olaf took him at his word. He stepped up the pace, thrusting into Paul's body and appreciating Paul's muscles tightening around him. His balls drew up, screaming their intention.

He looked at the clock. One minute.

"Ready?" he gasped out.

"Fuck yeah."

"Now!"

Olaf reached around and engulfed Paul's shaft in his large hand. Paul yelled and clenched around Olaf's cock.

They came together, Paul shuddering as Olaf gave the last few jerky thrusts and pushed in as hard as he could. Paul's arm gave out and Olaf tried to brace him so he didn't jar his injured arm. They ended up sprawled ungracefully over the desk, panting and laughing at the same time. By some miracle, Olaf was still inside Paul. He grabbed the box of tissues, also in the drawer, before it got messy.

Olaf looked at the clock as he zipped his pants. "I've got to get down there."

"I'm coming with you," Paul said.

"Like that?" Olaf queried.

Paul's sweats were around his knees. He hauled awkwardly with one hand. "You could help."

"I could," Olaf agreed, as he stepped forwards into Paul's space and pulled them up. "But I like watching you struggle."

"Useless boyfriend," Paul muttered.

"Wonderful fiancé," Olaf corrected. "And now we've got to go."

Paul handed him a notebook and pen. "At least try to look professional."

Wig raised an eyebrow as Olaf and Paul approached. "I didn't realise your office space included the restaurant." He sniffed the air delicately. "Seriously?"

"Is he here?" Olaf asked, ignoring the bitching and the unspoken question.

"He's over in the corner."

Olaf looked over to see a balding man in an England Rugby shirt, staring out of the window, tapping his fingers on the table.

"Has he ordered?"

"Not yet."

"I swear I know him," Paul mused.

"I'll leave you to think," Olaf said and hurried over to meet Tony Dobson.

"Mr Dobson?" he said as he reached the table.

The man looked at him and blanched. Olaf was used to that reaction. "Mr Skandik."

"Olaf please. I'm sorry if I kept you waiting."

He sat down as Wig came over to take their order. Most people meeting Wig for the first time at least blinked. Dobson did nothing. Just ordered a cup of tea and stared out the window again. Wig gave Olaf a meaningful look, and Olaf returned the merest of nods. Whatever was bothering Dobson, it was obviously consuming him.

Olaf waited for Wig to bring the drinks and leave them alone before he spoke. Dobson had not said a word.

"Mr Dobson, are you okay if I record our

meeting?" He caught the sudden suspicion in Dobson's expression. "What you tell me is confidential. I just don't want to be so busy making notes, I miss something important."

Dobson shrugged, but the tension didn't subside. "Go ahead. It's all old news."

If it was old news, why did Dobson look so scared at that moment?

As Olaf put his phone on the table and pressed play, he knew he had to handle his witness very carefully. "Bobby was your friend?"

"We were friends since playgroup. Went to the same schools. Hung out with the same crowd. Our dads worked together."

The pieces clicked together.

"Your dad was a cop?" Olaf asked.

"Yeah. All his working life."

"So you knew Robert Sargent too?"

Dobson smiled but it didn't reach his eyes. "Yeah. And before you ask, I knew exactly what he was like. Bobby was always covered in bruises. Keith too. And their mum. But no one gave a shit."

"Especially not the cops," Olaf suggested.

Dobson shrugged. "They closed ranks when it was one of their own."

"No one ever looked at Sargent for Bobby's disappearance?"

Dobson licked his lips as if he was suddenly nervous. "Not officially. But there was a reason Sargent never got promotion. He may not have been charged but they punished him all the same."

Interesting. Olaf had seen it done in the

sheriff's office. Olaf had had little time for the sheriff. He was a homophobic blowhard and still believed in the old boys' club. But when rumours surfaced about an officer abusing kids decades previously, the sheriff made sure the man never got any promotion he went for. He wouldn't sack the guy. The rumours were just that. But he punished him, nevertheless.

"Did Sargent know?"

"He knew," Dobson said shortly. "My dad said the man was too proud or too stupid to leave. He should have left the island, and we'd never have had to see his rotten heart again."

Olaf blinked as Dobson went back to watching the passers-by out the window. He sipped his coffee and thought about what to say next. "Mr Dobson, why are you so convinced Sargent killed Bobby? There's no evidence. No one ever found Bobby's body."

"They're not going to find him when he's at the bottom of the sea, are they?"

"That's what you think happened to him?"

"I know that's what happened to him."

"But no one saw Sargent kill Bobby, and your Dad could have seen Sargent just carrying an old rug to take to the dump."

"He was having a makeover in the middle of the night?" Dobson shot back.

Dobson had a point. Sargent could easily have disposed of the body at sea, and no one would have been any wiser.

"And he had a black eye the next day," Dobson added.

That matched up with Danny's version of events. Olaf wondered why Keith hadn't mentioned it.

"You think Bobby gave him that?"

Dobson nodded. "And then Sargent killed him."

"Is your dad still alive?" Olaf asked.

Dobson shook his head. "He died ten years ago. A heart attack."

"I'm sorry."

Damn, it would have been helpful to talk to a witness who was there.

"Me too," Dobson said.

Another long silence.

"Tell me about Bobby," Olaf suggested.

"What about him?" Dobson asked suspiciously.

"What was he like?"

"He was an arsehole."

Olaf blinked at Dobson's surprising honesty.

Dobson gave a humourless chuckle. "Don't get me wrong. I know Bobby was a nightmare. He was always fighting, even when he didn't have to. But he knew the world was against him."

"Because he was gay."

"Yeah. He was a good friend to me." Dobson went back to staring out the window.

Olaf wondered if there was anything else useful he could get from Dobson. The man seemed lost in his own world of hurt.

He was surprised when Wig fluttered over to them and dropped folded napkins in front of him.

"Sorry. I forgot to give you these." Then Wig fluttered away again.

As there were napkins on the table and they hadn't ordered food, this was clearly a ruse.

Tony pushed his to one side without a word.

Olaf opened his napkin.

Now I know! He's gay. Closet. Wife.

He could barely read Paul's scrawl, but the message was clear enough. More pieces fell into place.

Olaf fixed his attention on the man sitting opposite him. "Bobby was more than just a friend, wasn't he?"

Dobson's attention snapped back to him. "What do you mean?" His voice was raw and harsh.

"You loved him."

"No…I…how can you say that? I'm not a queer…how dare you—" Dobson looked around frantically, checking to see no one had overheard him.

Olaf cut him off before Dobson said something they'd both regret. "But I am, Mr Dobson. So don't waste my time or yours."

It was as if someone had stuck a pin in Dobson and he slumped in his chair. Olaf risked a quick glance at Paul and mouthed, "Thank you."

Paul gave him a sweet smile, but he looked worried. Olaf would pursue that later.

"How did you guess?" Dobson asked brokenly.

"I've been in the closet too," Olaf said, deflecting the question.

"I've never stepped out of it."

"You got married and had kids?"

Dobson nodded. "After what happened to Bobby, I was so damned scared. My dad…he was a good man, but he had the same views as Sargent on homos—gay men. I thought if Bobby's dad could kill him, maybe my dad would do the same to me. And then it was the AIDS epidemic, and any hope I had of coming out died. I got married at twenty. Had three kids by twenty-five."

Olaf could easily have followed the same path if he'd given in to his family's pressure. How did Paul know he was gay? Olaf took a stab in the dark.

"But you go to gay clubs?"

Dobson's eyes opened wide. "How did you know?" Then he turned and looked at Paul and back to Olaf. "Owens," he said without enthusiasm.

"You know Paul?"

"We fucked once or twice."

Olaf kept his face blank. He knew Paul's reputation before they'd met. He also knew Paul had been faithful to him since that day. It was always a shock when he met one of Paul's hook-ups, but it happened, and he'd learned to live with it.

But knowing this guy was unfaithful to his wife...was any of his information to be trusted? Or was that unfair? He'd known guys before who used clubs to let off steam. Olaf's mind was whirling. He wanted to say goodbye to Tony Dobson and talk to Paul.

As if Dobson overheard his thoughts, he looked at his watch. "I've got to go. I've got to get to work." He stood, paused, and gave Olaf a curious look. "You know Owens?"

"I do."

"You be careful with him. He's a manwhore."

Olaf gave him a tight smile. "Those days are behind him."

Dobson sneered. "That's what they all say."

Olaf took a deep breath before he was tempted to punch the guy on the nose. "I trust my fiancé, Mr Dobson." He took satisfaction in seeing Dobson's shocked expression. "Thanks for your information. You'd better get a move on if you're gonna get to work on time."

Dobson's eyes widened even more as Olaf stood and he realised just how tall Olaf was. Olaf could have ground him into beef. He disappeared out the door as if the hounds of hell were after him although Olaf didn't move a muscle.

"Let me guess. He told you we fucked," Paul murmured at his shoulder.

"He did," Olaf snapped. Then he fixed his gaze on Paul. "And I don't give a fuck about that, but no one gets to call you names—except me."

"And Sam and my brothers and—"

"No one," Olaf insisted. "You're mine."

Paul fluttered his eyelashes and placed his hand over his heart. "Be still my beating heart. You've gone all caveman on me."

Olaf grunted.

Paul chuckled. "You're the only one who's ever cared enough to defend my honour. But you don't have to do that, babe. I *was* a manwhore. Now I'm yours."

"Oh how sweet. I'm going to have cavities after that speech," Cameron said.

They turned to see Cameron and Jeff grinning

at them.

"Fuck off, Gillard," Paul groused, then pulled them both in for a hug.

"Ignore my husband," Jeff said to Olaf. "He's bitchy because I wouldn't let him play with Daisy this morning."

Paul furrowed his brow. "You've got a dog? I thought you were allergic, Cam?"

"I am. Daisy is Jeff's old car."

As Cameron was a car mechanic this made more sense.

"We had to clean the house," Jeff explained. "My mother is coming to stay, and half of Daisy's engine is spread over the downstairs of the cottage."

Olaf nodded. "I understand why you need to clean."

Cameron scowled at him. "You're not supposed to agree with him."

"Hi, guys."

Olaf grinned at Liam, and Sam and Nick and Logan joined them.

"You look exhausted," he said to Nick.

"I've not had much sleep. My husband dragged me out of my bed early."

Nick worked overnight on the fishing boats.

Logan kissed him on the cheek. "I'll make it up to you."

Nick's grumpy expression vanished into a gooey smile.

"Whipped," Paul crowed.

Olaf raised an eyebrow at him, and he subsided.

"You've got to teach me how you do that," Sam insisted. "You and Liam are the only ones who keep Paul under control."

Paul flipped him off.

"Guys, sit down," Wig ordered. "You're making the place look untidy."

They sat at their usual round table, chattering loudly, content to be in each other's company. Olaf looked around at his friends. He thought of Tony Dobson and the bitterness that consumed him.

He tugged Paul closer and muttered in his ear, "I was so lucky to meet you."

Under the bruising Paul gave him a brilliant smile. "I know."

Olaf snorted as the others pelted Paul with bread, to Wig's disgust. Paul would never change. Olaf never wanted him to.

Chapter 11

Saturday

They stayed at the Lagoon late into the evening. Nick had a night off, and Jeff wasn't on call. Wig and Nibs joined them when the restaurant closed. It was good to spend time together and Olaf relaxed in a way he only did when he was around these eight men who had become the closest friends he'd ever had. Paul dozed off as the night progressed, sleeping against Olaf's chest.

"How's he doing?" Logan asked quietly. Olaf bit his lip and Logan nodded. "Bring him over soon. Really soon."

"He won't agree."

Liam leaned forwards. "He will. I'll talk to him."

The guys went silent for a moment, and Liam rolled his eyes.

Olaf grinned at him. "You know they're trying to think of something kind to say to you."

"I know," Liam sighed. "Seriously, guys, you can quit treading on eggshells around me. I'm all good."

"He's just fine." Sam leered at him.

Olaf noticed Logan said nothing, but maybe that was a professional thing. He did know that if it hadn't been for Logan, Liam might not have been sitting here today.

"The alternative is he talks to me," Jeff said. He rolled his eyes as Logan shuddered. "I'm not that bad."

"You're worse," Logan said, "but I love you."

Nick raised an eyebrow. "Is there something Cam and I should know?"

They both flipped him off.

"Charming," Nick muttered, then smirked at them.

Paul sighed and burrowed into Olaf who kissed the top of his head.

"I'll take him home," Olaf said. "It's been a long day."

"Has he made up his mind about the promotion?" Nibs asked.

Olaf was surprised that Nibs, who tended to be on the outskirts of the group simply because of the long hours he worked, knew about the promotion.

"Not yet." Olaf didn't want to think about it.

"You tie him to the bed and make him stay here," Nibs advised.

Olaf smiled at him. "I think I might just do that."

Paul raised his head, blinking at him sleepily. "You're the one tied to the bed, remember?"

It was a measure of how well they all knew each other that this comment didn't even merit a lull in the conversation.

"I think it's time that changed," Olaf whispered in his ear, loving Paul's shudder. "Let's go home."

Paul sat up and knuckled his eyes. "How long was I asleep?"

"About an hour."

"Damn, sorry guys. I can't wait for this to be over."

"You've got to give yourself a chance to heal," Nick said.

Liam and Logan nodded.

"As a group we've spent more than our fair share of time bruised and battered," Liam laughed.

"Do you remember that patient who smacked you in the face?" Cameron asked Jeff.

"Or the arseholes who pushed you down the stairs," Jeff responded.

Olaf stood and took Paul with him. "I'll leave you to compare injuries. I'm taking my boy home."

They were hugged and kissed. Logan hugged him with a muttered, "Soon, you hear?"

"I promise," Olaf agreed. If Logan was worried enough about Paul to insist, he would obey.

Liam took Paul to one side and spoke to him. Olaf saw Paul's eyebrows knit, and his expression grew mutinous, but Liam kept talking and finally Paul sighed and nodded. Olaf breathed easier. Paul would do anything to make his brother-in-law happy.

They were walking to the car, Olaf's arm around Paul's shoulders, when Paul said, "Did you get ambushed too?"

"Yeah, while you were asleep."

"Do you think I need to talk to Logan?"

"You're friends so I don't know if you can talk to him formally, but maybe just a chat? Reassure them all. You know they won't let it go otherwise."

"You haven't answered the question."

"I don't think it's the assault that's affecting you as much as the promotion offer," Olaf said finally. "I think that's making you conflicted."

Paul was silent for a long moment. "Yeah, you're right. Logan's a decent shrink, but I don't need him to tell me what's keeping me awake at night."

Olaf stopped and tilted Paul's chin up to look at him. "You've not been sleeping at night?"

"On and off. I caught up during the day with all those naps."

The way Paul refused to meet his gaze told Olaf it had been more off than on.

"You should have woken me up," Olaf chided.

Paul shrugged. "Then two of us wouldn't be sleeping, and you've got a missing man to find. Come on, let's go home."

Olaf hummed as they started walking again. "Tony Dobson."

"Yeah?"

"What do you make of him?"

"Closet case," Paul said promptly. "Wondering where his life has gone wrong. Angry all the time."

"Yeah, that's the impression I got too."

"And really, really scared."

"What's he scared of?" Olaf asked.

They'd reached the car by this time and Paul waited until they were both seated before he answered. "Losing his family. I don't know him well, but Biggsy does, and he's devoted to his kids. And from what I hear he's good to his wife."

"So he hides all that anger and pain from them?"

"Maybe he shows it to us because he knows we'll understand."

Olaf glanced at Paul. "That's very perceptive of you."

"I have my moments." Paul leaned back against the seat and sighed. "He was always scared of being discovered. I'm surprised he even admitted he was gay to you."

"I told him I was gay before he launched into the tirade," Olaf said dryly. "I get the feeling that discovering Keith is looking for his brother is adding additional stress. He's been convinced for so long that Sargent killed the boy he loved, the idea that Bobby could still be alive is making him unravel."

"He loved Bobby?" Paul exclaimed.

"Yes. Although I don't know if it was returned."

"Ouch. Poor bastard. No wonder he's falling apart."

"We still don't know one way or the other. I'll chase Reynolds at the end of the week." It was the one thread Olaf couldn't tie up.

"Good idea."

"Paul."

"Hmm?" Paul sounded sleepy again.

Olaf placed a hand briefly on Paul's thigh. "If you wake up during the night, make sure you wake me up, yeah?"

"I promise."

"You'd better not be crossing your fingers," Olaf said.

He received a snore in response.

Back at home, Olaf steered Paul into the bedroom, untangled him from his sling, undressed him and eased him under the duvet. He was asleep again in seconds. Olaf envied him. He was tired, but not enough to sleep. He bent and kissed Paul on the forehead, the only part of him visible.

Olaf made himself a hot chocolate and sat on his couch to listen to Dobson's heated words. Something Dobson had said bothered him, but he couldn't tease out what it was. The rational part of Olaf didn't put much stock in the idea of Sargent's night-time flit to the bay. Dobson had been a hormonal teenage boy with a secret crush on his friend. Believing Sargent had killed his friend probably satisfied the angry part of him. On the other hand, Sargent's co-workers had clearly suspected him of the same thing because of the way he was treated afterwards.

Olaf grabbed a notebook and pen on the coffee table and made a note to talk to Daniel Gillard. If Daniel confirmed Dobson's story, then Olaf would pursue that line of enquiry. Another thought occurred to him. What happened to Sargent's boat? He made another note to ask Keith.

He looked up as Paul stood in the doorway, his eyes barely open, his hair sticking up in all directions.

"Are you all right, sweetheart? Do you need

painkillers?"

"Need you to come to bed," Paul murmured. "Can't sleep without my fuzzy pillow."

Olaf downed the hot chocolate and stood, taking Paul's hand. "Okay, but if you wake up in the night, you wake me too, yes?"

Paul murmured something incoherent. It could have been yes or no. Olaf decided not to push it.

He stripped down to his briefs and climbed into bed. They'd swapped sides so Paul could rest his injured arm on Olaf's body. Olaf realised how much he missed the feel of Paul's soft skin rather than the rough covering of the cast.

Paul gave a happy sigh as he settled against Olaf. "Better," he declared.

Olaf brushed a kiss on his forehead. "Sleep tight, sweetheart."

He wasn't sure when he'd started calling his spiky, feisty lover, his sweetheart. Initially it had been to annoy Paul, but when he saw Paul just melted every time Olaf used it, sweetheart had stayed. He had never called anyone else his sweetheart and he'd been sure he never would.

Olaf expected to stay awake, thinking about the case, but to his relief, sleep came easily as Paul snored in his arms.

Sunday

Waking was not so easy. Olaf was deep in a dream about sneaking away in the middle of the night, Paul wrapped in a rug over his shoulder, when something hard hit him on the nose.

"Ouch!" he yelled.

"Fuck!"

Olaf opened his eyes to find Paul curled over himself, nursing his arm. He sat up and put his arm around Paul's shoulders. "What just happened?"

Paul took a moment to answer. Olaf rubbed slow, soothing circles on his back. "I was dreaming you were trying to kidnap me. In my dream I hit you to get away, but it hurt like hell." He glanced at Olaf. "Your nose is bleeding."

Olaf touched his nose, then looked at his fingers coated in blood. "Damn." He grabbed the tissues on the shelf. "You must have hit me with your cast. Are you okay?" The last sentence was muffled as he tried to stem the flow of blood.

Paul flexed his fingers carefully. "I think so. It was more the shock."

"I dreamt I was sneaking away in the night with you over my shoulder in a rug," Olaf confessed.

"No prizes for guessing where these dreams came from," Paul said ruefully. "How's your nose?"

"Sore, but I think the bleeding has stopped. How does it look?"

Paul studied him. "It's a pity it's not panto season."

Olaf stared at him blankly. "Huh?"

"You could audition for the part of Rudolph the red-nosed reindeer in a pantomime."

Olaf touched his tender nose. "You mean it's red?"

"Glowing," Paul assured him.

"People are going to think we beat each other,"

Olaf muttered.

Paul shivered. "That's the last thing we need, especially with this case."

"You're looking better. The bruising is starting to fade here." Olaf brushed the area lightly with his fingers. He knew Paul had struggled with the way he looked. His boy was a little—okay, a lot—vain. Like his brothers, Paul was handsome with an edge of pretty. Olaf knew exactly what Paul would look like as he grew older. Now he didn't dye his hair, he was the mirror image of his older brothers and his father. Paul had struggled with reaching thirty, but one memorable night looking in the mirror, as Olaf pointed out everything about Paul that made him hard, had gone a long way to convincing him how gorgeous he still was. Paul had taken his time but finally realised that, although he couldn't be the prettiest boy in the room anymore, he could be Olaf's. Olaf understood. He'd gotten over his aging moment before he met Paul. He was blessed with his Slavic features, but he was now mid-forties, and the lines around his eyes had deepened over the years, and his hair was more ash than blond. Even the fuzz that Paul was so obsessed by was fading in colour. But overall, they were two good-looking, middle-aged men, or they would be once Paul's bruising had faded.

"What time is it?" Paul asked.

Olaf looked at his phone. "Six-thirty."

Paul flopped back onto the pillows, wincing as he jarred his arm again. "Damn, it's too early to get up."

"Are you sleepy?" Olaf asked.

"What are you thinking?"

"I make you a cup of tea and we cuddle and catch up on the TV we missed last night?"

Paul groaned. "If you'd asked me that a few weeks ago I'd have been offended."

"But now it's just what you want?" Olaf said.

"It's just what I need. You and me and *After Life*."

Olaf climbed out of bed. "Ten minutes and I'll be back."

"You could make toast too," Paul suggested.

Olaf raised an eyebrow. "Any other orders?"

Paul thought for a moment. "No, that'll be good."

Olaf waited.

"Maybe a banana...and a yoghurt." Paul tapped his chin. "Do we have any pastries left?"

"I'm going," Olaf said, before Paul asked for eggs and bacon too.

He stopped via the bathroom and looked at the damage to his nose. It was pink but not swollen. He could pass on the role of Rudolph this time.

In the kitchen Olaf prepared a breakfast fit for his lover. It wasn't often they got a chance to laze in bed together. Even when Paul was here, Olaf was usually working. This was a treat he wouldn't pass up. He wasn't surprised to find Paul dozing but he woke as Olaf walked into the room.

"Did I fall asleep again?"

"Yup. You're safe. I didn't take a photo of you drooling."

"Up yours, Skandik," Paul said sourly. He

looked adorable, all sleepy and pouty.

Olaf chuckled and placed the tray on Paul's lap. "This is yours. I'll be back in a moment."

He returned to the kitchen to get his tray. When he came back Paul had switched on the TV and was watching the news intently.

"Anything interesting?" Olaf asked.

"Tony Dobson got arrested last night."

"What for?"

"He got plastered and picked a fight."

Olaf sighed. "Dammit, I'd never have agreed to see him if he was going to go off the rails."

"I'll talk with Biggsy later." Paul picked up the toast. "They might just leave him to sleep it off."

"He was in love with Bobby," Olaf said as he carefully wriggled under the duvet.

"You said that yesterday. Poor bastard. No wonder he's conflicted, but he's not gonna keep his home life if he keeps picking fights. He'll get drunk and it will all come out."

"I've got to call Cam's dad later. Maybe he can have a word with him. Calm him down." Olaf picked up his coffee. "Okay, TV and food. I don't want to think about Dobson or Sargent or anyone except you for a couple of hours."

Paul sighed. "That sounds good to me."

Olaf was making notes at the table when Paul came in.

"Could you drop me off at Logan's?" Paul asked.

"Sure. Now?"

Olaf was surprised. Paul had seemed so against

the idea of talking to Logan the previous night.

Paul grimaced. "Logan called me. I tried to get out of it, but he insisted."

"Okay." Olaf would have to thank Logan later.

"I would have told him to fuck off, but..."

Olaf looked at him curiously. "But?"

Paul sat down opposite him. "Liam told me I needed to pull my head out of my arse."

Olaf tried to hide his smile but he obviously failed when Paul rolled his eyes.

"Yeah, yeah, I know," Paul groused. "You don't need to say it."

Olaf leaned back in the chair. "Liam loves you, and he wants you to be happy. Logan's the same."

Paul frowned. "They don't think I'm happy? Do *you* think I'm happy?"

Olaf was suddenly aware of the quicksand ahead of him. "I think you don't know what you want."

"You're right. I mean, I know I want you. That's never in doubt."

"That's sweet and you know I feel the same about you. But promotion is all you've ever aimed for."

"Yes."

"Just not this promotion," Olaf said softly.

"Yes," Paul agreed.

"Keep our friends happy. Talk to Logan. I've talked to him in the past."

Paul blinked. "You have? You never told me."

"I needed to sort out some shit in my head. Nick was working. Logan invited me around for dinner. Before I knew it, I was spilling my guts out over the chicken fajitas."

"He's sneaky like that," Paul said.

"Logan is, but he's damn good at it. We—I—talked for hours, but by the end of it, I felt better, more focused. If he can do that for you, quit complaining."

Paul gave him a long look "Was I the shit in your head?"

"Some," Olaf agreed. "Not all."

"And Logan helped?"

"He did."

If it hadn't been for Logan, Olaf would have boarded the plane to Kelder. He'd already gotten the tickets.

Paul nodded. "Okay then. Maybe he can do the same for me."

Olaf got to his feet. "Give me one moment to finish my notes, and I'll drive you there."

"I wonder how many secrets Logan knows about us all."

"Too many," Olaf smirked. "But he still loves us."

Chapter 12

Monday

Olaf pushed open the door of the Blue Lagoon, hoping for breakfast and a chance to relax before the week began. Wig swayed over to him to receive his hug. This was his due, and Olaf gave it willingly, enfolding the smaller man in his arms and kissing his cheek.

"Where's your boy?" Wig demanded.

"I don't know," Olaf admitted. "He wouldn't tell me. He was cagey about it. I guess he might be going to see Logan again. But he's going to meet me here later for lunch. I need coffee and breakfast."

"You're never going to make any money if you keep spending it in here," Wig pointed out.

"Maybe we could work out a deal."

"Uh-huh," Wig drawled. "Good luck with that one. Sit down and I'll bring the coffee pot."

"You could leave it with me," Olaf suggested.

Wig ignored him.

Olaf grinned and went to sit in his usual seat. He appreciated the time to think, although he did more staring out the window than actual thinking.

While he was waiting for the coffee, he sent a quick text to Daniel Gillard asking if he could call him in about an hour. He received an immediate response.

"Sure."

Olaf breathed easier. He was still waiting to hear from the Reynolds agency, but he could chase them later in the week.

"Nibs says make sure you give him a kiss too." Wig grinned as he poured the cup of the fragrant brew. "He was jealous."

Olaf rolled his eyes. "You're just winding him up."

"Of course I am," Wig said haughtily. "He needs reminding other men like giving me a kiss."

Olaf was used to Wig and Nibs's games. Yes, Wig liked being hugged and kissed, but only within their circle of friends, and there was kissing, and *kissing*.

"He worships the ground you walk on," Olaf said.

"As he should," Wig assured him.

Olaf grinned as Wig went to greet new customers. Wig would never change.

Daniel sighed down the phone when Olaf explained about Tony Dobson. "I had a feeling at the time, but he was a quiet kid, and we weren't close friends. I never spoke to him again after Bobby disappeared."

"I think he could do with a friend now or he's going to fuck up his life. Sorry, sir," Olaf said. "And you knew Bobby."

"I understand, and don't call me sir. That makes me feel old."

"Force of habit," Olaf murmured. He was much closer in age to Daniel than Cam, yet Cam was his friend.

"I'll talk to Tony," Daniel said. "Have you got any further with the case?"

"Not really. There are lots of threads but nothing much to tie them together at the moment."

"It's odd. Bobby's been gone most of my life yet he's still so sharp in my mind. He was like the sun, you know? Someone you'd never forget." Daniel sounded almost wistful.

"Unlike Tony Dobson."

"Unlike Tony," Daniel agreed. "Leave it with me, Olaf. I'll talk to Tony. I can't promise anything, but if he needs a shoulder, he'll know where to come."

"Thanks, sir—Daniel."

That left Olaf with not a lot to do except think, and the phone was a welcome interruption. He connected the call without checking to see who it was.

"Mr Skandik?"

The male voice was unfamiliar, brusque but friendly.

"I'm Olaf Skandik," Olaf said. "How may I help you?"

"It's David Reynolds from Stuart Reynolds Investigators. Sorry for the delay in getting back to you, but Uncle Stuart's records were a mess, and we haven't got around to digitising his cases."

Olaf perked up. "Did you find something?"

"I did, such as it is."

Olaf's heart sank.

"Mr Skandik, do you have time to visit me? Normally I'd courier it but we're talking a couple of pages at the most. Uncle Stuart was an old-fashioned man, and he didn't believe in making notes. I could scan you the notes, but I remember this case."

"You do?"

"I was a kid at the time, but a local lad going missing was a big deal, and I remember my uncle talking to my parents about the case. I think you'll be interested in what I have to say. Are you free this afternoon?"

Olaf looked at the clock. It was still only nine-thirty. He'd promised to meet Paul for lunch but maybe Paul could make it early. "Yes, I am. About two?"

"Make it two-thirty. I've got a meeting at one."

"Two-thirty it is. You're in Portsmouth now?"

"Yes, I am. You can walk to my office from the Catamaran terminal."

"Great. I'll see you then."

There was a long silence, and Olaf waited, sensing that Reynolds had something else to say.

"You know, I was pleased when you contacted me," Reynolds said finally. "When I heard Sargent had died, I had a feeling Keith would try to find his brother. I've never forgotten Bobby Sargent."

"Keith approached your agency," Olaf pointed out, remembering what Keith had said.

"I didn't know that," Reynolds murmured. "I don't handle new cases. Well, see you later."

As soon as he disconnected from Reynolds, Olaf called Paul.

"Morning, babe," Paul said cheerfully. "Is everything okay?"

"Yeah. I've got to go over to the mainland for two-thirty. The guy from Stuart Reynolds contacted me. Do you have time for an early lunch? Say eleven at Ryde?"

"Sure. Or I could come over with you and we'll get lunch at the Spinnaker. I can wait while you have your meeting."

That was even better. It would do them both good to get a change of scene.

"Do you want me to pick you up?" Olaf asked.

"Hold on."

Olaf frowned as he heard Paul talking to someone. Where was he?

"Olaf? Jeff's going to drop me at the office around eleven. We're just in the middle of a cooking lesson."

"You're learning to cook?" Olaf asked doubtfully.

"Thanks for your vote of confidence, babe."

Olaf wisely ignored that. "Cam's not supervising, is he?"

Paul snickered. "I told Jeff you'd ask that. Cam's safely at work. I just wanted the recipe for the chicken pot pie he served the last time we were there. And he suggested he taught me how to cook it. I can drop it at home and then come to you."

"You don't have to rush. I could go by myself."

"Jeff's got to work later this morning. It's why I went early. I'll see you about eleven."

Olaf grinned as he disconnected the call. So that's why his boy had been cagey. He was learning to cook. What would he do until Paul arrived?

Research. He needed a website for the business. He decided to look at other private investigator businesses for ideas.

By the time Paul arrived, Olaf was cross-eyed and desperate for a distraction. Paul had barely set a foot in the room before Olaf was out of his seat and rushing over to cuddle him.

"Whoa!" Paul said, his voice somewhat muffled from his face buried in Olaf's shoulder. "What's wrong with you?"

"What the hell did I think I was doing?" Olaf blurted out. "I can't be a private investigator. I don't have access to forensic labs and international contacts and other shit." He stepped back and glared at Paul. "What were you thinking, agreeing to this?"

"You resigned before you talked to me, remember?" Paul pointed out.

"I know!" Olaf wailed. "What was I thinking?"

"Okay, babe, sit down before you fall down. If you pass out in here, you'll take me with you. Tell me what's got you freaked out."

Olaf stalked over to the desk and turned his laptop to face Paul. "This!"

Paul peered at the screen. "Cranky & Dashing Private Investigators. Christ, they sound like something out of Victorian era. Look like it too. Is that guy wearing a bowler hat?"

"And this." Olaf clicked to another one.

"QuickFire Investigators." Paul furrowed his brow. "I know them. I don't know why."

Another click. "And this one."

"Angel Enterprises. That website is a bit sparse."

"No, that's not the one I mean. This one." Olaf showed him the website for Stuart Reynolds.

Paul rubbed Olaf's arm. "These are established businesses, Olaf. You haven't got started yet."

"I know that, but the more I look at these the more I realise I'm out of my depth. What can I offer anyone?"

"Nearly twenty years of police experience," Paul suggested. "A compassionate nature. You're a crack detective."

"Yes, but that's just me."

"Take a deep breath before you pass out. You haven't even officially started yet. You didn't expect to get your first case before you advertised, but you've already got money in the bank. Yes, you need a website, but I've got that sorted."

"You have?" Olaf asked warily.

"Steve from downstairs said he'll do it for you. Turns out the fry cook is a whizz with websites."

"Good alliteration," Olaf muttered.

"What? Never mind. I've been meaning to tell you this for weeks, but I got distracted by this." Paul pointed to the cast.

Olaf nodded absently. "I should have thought of it sooner. Christ, I'm so unprepared for this."

"We both are, but you know, you've hit the ground running. Let's go to lunch and we can discuss what you need on the website."

Olaf took that deep breath Paul suggested and then another one. He needed to get a grip. Solve this case and then he'd have more time to worry about the business. This case had been a one off. It wasn't like he was going to get more work immediately.

He forced a smile at Paul. "The catamaran, then lunch. I might calm down by the time we reach Portsmouth."

"It's not like you to panic," Paul observed as Olaf shut his laptop and made sure he had everything he needed.

"I was fine until I looked at the competition."

"I understand that. But don't panic yet. Maybe this Reynolds guy could give you a few pointers."

"Have you seen his website?" Olaf felt the panic rising again.

Paul snorted. "Okay, take a deep breath. Let's get out of here."

It was a good suggestion and Olaf felt his panic fading as he waited for the catamaran. It was ridiculous to get so worked up. As Paul said, he'd barely gotten his boots wet. He gave Paul a wry smile. "Sorry for being an idiot."

Paul squeezed his hand. "Don't worry about anything except finding Bobby Sargent."

"Cam's dad is going to talk to Dobson."

"Knowing them, he'll be brought into the family."

Olaf frowned. "The Gillards?"

"More like the island collective," Paul said.

A thought occurred to Olaf. "Do you think your parents will move down here?"

"I don't think so. Dad's talked about it before but Mum likes living in London. Her whole life is there, including the family except Sam. She misses Sam, but now Colin and Dan have babies she's distracted."

"At least your parents aren't bothered about more grandchildren."

Olaf tried not to sound bitter. He knew it was another disappointment in a long line of disappointments he'd inflicted on his parents. No baby Skandiks. He'd tried to explain to his mom that he'd never wanted kids anyway, but she felt it was his duty to carry on the family line.

"Hey," Paul said softly. "I love you."

Olaf smiled at him. "How do you always know what to say to make me feel better?"

"I speak Olaf."

They locked gazes and Olaf was on the point of drawing Paul into his arms when Paul lurched forwards, crashing into Olaf's solid body.

"Sorry, mate."

Olaf ignored the apology behind Paul and focused on steadying him, holding Paul's upper arms. "Are you okay?"

From the tightness around Paul's mouth and eyes, he was clearly not okay, but he said, "Yeah. It was just a surprise."

"Is your arm okay?"

"Throbbing," Paul admitted. "That hurt like hell."

Olaf glared at the man over the top of Paul's head and then he realised who it was. Recognition dawned in Tony Dobson's eyes.

"Sorry, Owens," he muttered. "I didn't mean to knock you."

"It was my fault," a woman said, looking apologetic. "I slipped and fell against Tony. Do you know each other? Wait, aren't you one of Rose's grandkids?"

Paul forced a smile even though Olaf could see he was in pain. "I am. I'm Paul Owens. You must be Tony's wife."

"That's right. I'm Kim. I met Rose in hospital." She beamed at him, then she spotted his sling and her smile faded. "Gosh, what happened to your arm?"

"I'm a police officer. It happens."

Kim looked curiously at Olaf. "I don't know you."

"He's my fiancé," Paul said.

Olaf held out his hand. "Olaf Skandik."

Her eyes opened wide. "American."

"How did you guess?" Olaf smiled to lessen the sarcasm.

"And you're from...let me guess...Wisconsin?"

Despite himself, Olaf was impressed. "How did you know that?"

Kim reddened. "I'd like to pretend I guessed your accent, but actually I think Charley Gillard told me."

Olaf laughed. "There are no secrets here." Then he felt bad because he knew a secret that could detonate her world, but he liked Kim Dobson. She seemed like a nice person. He could see the panic in Tony's eyes, but he kept his focus on Kim, not wanting to give any hint he was talking about anything else than his past.

"We should go," Paul murmured.

"Okay then. Good to meet you, Kim. Dobson."

He nodded at them both and guided Paul away towards the catamaran. He let out a breath when they were out of earshot.

"Well, that was awkward," Paul murmured.

"Just a bit. Is there somewhere we can hide?"

"We'll find somewhere," Paul promised.

"I need your arms, good food, and then David Reynolds to tell me something that will help me solve my case."

Paul smirked at him. "Not asking for a lot, are you? You get one arm from me."

"I don't think so." Olaf looked down at Paul. "How's your bad arm now?"

"I'd like to curl up in a corner and cry," Paul admitted. "You've got a hard chest."

"Sorry about that. I thought you liked my chest."

"I do. But if I'd fallen against Nibs, it would have been softer."

"He is one big bear," Olaf agreed. "Do you need to see a doctor?"

"No." Paul wiggled his fingers. "Nothing broken—again."

They found a seat and stretched out, Olaf holding Paul to him. He still freaked at showing affection in public but, right this second, he needed Paul close to him. They got a few looks, but no one bothered them. It was useful being six foot five with a stern look. They were left alone apart from a few people who recognised them both.

He rested his cheek on Paul's head. "Love you," he murmured.

Paul settled against him with a sigh. "Love you too."

Olaf stared up at the shiny glass and chrome building with the Stuart Reynolds logo everywhere. "Fuck."

"Meh. It's just a building." Paul shrugged. Then winced. "I really shouldn't have done that. Go talk to him. I'm going to have a beer."

"I think I'd rather have the beer."

Paul nudged him. "Go be the big bad detective."

"I *was* the big bad detective. Now I'm not sure what I am," Olaf admitted.

"Just go. I'll be waiting for you."

Olaf could hear the edge of impatience in Paul's voice. He sucked in a breath, straightened his shoulders, and strode into the building. A woman at the desk gave him a professional smile.

"May I help you?"

"I'm here to see David Reynolds."

"Mr Skandik?"

"Yes, that's right."

"He's expecting you. Take the lift to the seventh floor. Someone will meet you."

Olaf walked to the elevator and pressed the button. At the seventh floor he got out to be met by a handsome, dark-haired man he'd seen on the website. He knew Reynolds was the same age as him.

"Mr Reynolds?" he asked.

"David, please. It gets confusing with all the Reynolds's working here."

Olaf laughed and relaxed. "My life is like that."

"You live on the Isle of Wight, don't you?"

"I do."

Reynolds led him down the corridor to a corner office. It was functional rather than designed to impress. Olaf gathered from the screens on the desk that Reynolds was more interested in the tech than the decoration. He was obviously a hands-on employer.

"Coffee?"

"Yes please."

There was a machine in the room and, in a few minutes, both of them had a cup in front of them.

Reynolds sat behind his desk and pushed a thin folder over to Olaf. "These are all the notes we have on Bobby Sargent."

Olaf picked up the folder and opened it, revealing two sparsely handwritten sheets. "This is it?" he asked in dismay.

"This is it. I told you Uncle Stuart didn't bother with notes. And don't get me wrong. If our client, Robert Sargent, had still been alive, you wouldn't be looking at these."

"I understand."

"You don't yet, but you will do." Reynolds smiled at him. "I know the rumours, Olaf. May I call you Olaf?" At Olaf's nod, he continued. "I may not be on the island, but I have family over there. My brother lives just down the road from Robert Sargent. Sargent picked my uncle because they played darts together. Stuart was a bloody useless PI, to be honest."

Olaf looked at him in confusion. "Then why use his name? Why not your name?"

"It was a fuck you to my dad. The stupid things we do when we're first starting out. I plan to change the name soon. But, as I was saying, Stuart was useless, but he often talked through cases with his brother, my dad."

"Including this case."

"Yes. He was troubled. You see he knew about Bobby. Knew he was gay. And Bobby was a right pain in the arse."

Olaf smiled at him. "So everyone tells me."

"But he also knew Sargent was abusive, and my uncle hated the idea that Bobby would be taken back to that home. My uncle believed Sargent would kill Bobby if he got his hands on him."

Olaf had a glimmer of light as to where this was leading. "Are you saying he knew Bobby was alive all this time?"

Reynolds looked him in the eye. "Yes, he did. And he never told Sargent. As far as he was concerned, Stuart never found Bobby Reynolds. He didn't want Sargent anywhere near his son."

Olaf stared at him. "You know what you're telling me."

"That Bobby Sargent is alive."

At the beginning, he'd thought Reynolds wouldn't give him the information if Sargent had been alive because he was the client. But no, it was to protect Bobby.

"Do you have Bobby's address?"

Reynolds's lips twitched. "You're the detective. You find it."

Tuesday

For most of Tuesday, Olaf and Paul sat with their laptops and did what Reynolds had told Olaf to do. They hunted for Bobby Sargent.

"Of course, he might have died since then," Paul suggested.

"No. Reynolds knows he's alive. I'm damned sure he knows where he is, but he's not being paid. I am. He's not going to do my work for me."

"What does that say?" Olaf asked, pointing to a scrawl on the second page.

Paul squinted at it. "*Am wrong*? Wrong about what?"

"Not giving Robert the information maybe?"

Olaf pursed his lips. "Maybe."

Paul twisted the page around to face him. "Am wrong. Am wrong. No, that's not right. I think it could be Armstrong. That could be an s and a t."

Olaf was dubious but it was a name at least.

"Armstrong has to mean something," Paul said. "And look, that's a Southampton postcode."

"I'll look it up." Olaf typed the postcode into Google. "There used to be a business at one of the addresses run by Jack Armstrong, but it's wound up."

Yes! Excitement started to build in Olaf. They were so close. He could feel it.

"Perhaps Bobby changed his name to Jack Armstrong," Paul suggested.

"Or it could be a boyfriend."

Paul made a choking noise.

"What's wrong?" Olaf asked.

"No fucking way. No fucking way." Paul sounded almost giddy.

"What?"

"I just looked up Jack Armstrong on Facebook."

Paul turned the laptop to show Olaf. Two middle-aged men stared at them, dressed in tuxes with boutonnieres. Both smiling as if this was the happiest day of their lives.

"Who are they?"

"Jack and…Rob Armstrong. We've found them. We've fucking found them!"

Paul turned the laptop back to face him. "They live in Fulham. And you'll never guess what. Jack Armstrong runs a business, and we've got his address. We've fucking got his address."

Olaf stood to look over Paul's shoulder. "Which one's Rob?"

"That one," Paul said, pointed to the taller, almost white-haired man. This is our guy."

Olaf studied him for a moment. There was little left of the fresh-faced teen they'd been hunting for, except perhaps the mischievous twinkle in his eyes.

"You know what this means, don't you?" he said.

"You can tell Keith his father didn't murder his brother?"

"Well, yes, but first, fancy a roadtrip?"

Chapter 13

Wednesday

Olaf parked outside the small, terraced house in Fulham. He turned to look at Paul who seemed as troubled as he was, judging by his expression. They had both been silent for most of the journey. Olaf sighed and rubbed his scalp. "What if we're opening a whole can of worms Bobby Sargent doesn't want opened?"

Paul pressed his lips together. "All we have to do is find out if this is Bobby. We don't have to give Keith his address if Bobby says no. Keith only wanted to find out what happened to his brother."

Olaf gave him a sceptical look. "Would that be enough for you? If you found out one of your brothers was alive after thirty-five years? Would you be content to leave it there?"

"No," Paul admitted. "I'd do everything in my power to find him again. But that's not our problem. Let's get it over with."

They got out of the car and looked at the house. Bright red geraniums tumbled from window boxes and there were more flowers in pots either side of the path.

"Another Sargent who likes gardening?" Paul murmured.

Olaf pressed the doorbell.

"Coming," a male voice said inside.

The door opened and Olaf blinked at the short, grey-haired man dressed in a tight long-sleeved T-shirt and jeans who smiled at them. This was the guy from the Facebook photo. "Yes?"

"Are you Bobby Sargent?" Olaf asked, even knowing he wasn't.

The man stiffened and he clutched at the door frame.

Bingo.

But the man said, "No. There's no one of that name here."

"You know the name, though. Don't you?" Paul said softly.

"No, I don't know anyone of that name. I'm sorry." He went to shut the door, but just then Olaf spotted another man coming down the stairs wearing only a pair of jeans. Tall, white as snow hair, including the patch on his chest. This was his quarry. He'd been handsome in the photo, but he was gorgeous in real life.

"Hey, do you know where my blue shirt is, Jack?" the man asked, seemingly oblivious to the tension at the door. He looked up and saw Olaf and Paul. "Oh, hi. Can we help you?"

"Bobby Sargent?" Olaf asked.

The colour drained out of the man's face, and he swayed. "Jack," he whispered.

Jack rushed over and wrapped his arm around Bobby's—because it was obvious now—waist and held him close. He glared angrily at Olaf and Paul. "We don't know anyone by that name."

"Maybe not now, but once upon a time?" Paul said. Olaf could hear the compassion in his voice.

"How did you find me?" Bobby said.

Olaf breathed a sigh of relief that they were giving up the bullshit. "It's a long story, sir. Please may we come in?"

"Rob—" Jack started but Bobby shook his head.

"We always knew this day would come, Jack. Let them talk."

Jack didn't look convinced, but to Olaf's relief, he stood back and let them over the threshold.

"Come into the kitchen," Bobby said.

"Put a shirt on," Jack snapped. "The blue one is in the front room."

Bobby nodded and disappeared through the nearest doorway, leaving Jack glaring at them. It was easy to see he was freaked by their appearance, whereas Bobby seemed more resigned.

Bobby reappeared, buttoning the shirt, and led the way into the kitchen.

"Do you want a cup of tea or coffee?" he asked.

"Tea for me, coffee for him. Thanks," Paul said.

"Before you give them anything, I want to know who you are," Jack demanded.

"My name is Olaf Skandik. I'm a private investigator," Olaf said. "And this is my partner, Paul Owens."

"Business or life partner?" Bobby asked.

"Paul is my fiancé."

Bobby studied Paul's face. "Is Olaf free with his fists too?"

Just the phrase they'd used about Robert

Sargent. Any doubts about who he was were rapidly diminishing.

Before Olaf could protest about his assumption, Paul shook his head. "Got this because I stepped in front of a drunk bloke at work."

Bobby turned to Olaf. "Sorry. I had to ask." Then he narrowed his eyes and he turned back to Paul. "Owens. Any relation to Jim?"

Paul grinned. "He's my dad."

"I should have guessed. You look like him. Same eyes. Rose must have been your gran."

Olaf saw the look of sadness on Paul's face, but he just nodded. "She was. She died a few years ago."

"I'm sorry." Bobby sounded genuine. "I liked Rose a lot. We used to play in her back garden." He took a deep breath. "So why are you here? Did my dad send you?"

Olaf hesitated. It wasn't that he'd never delivered bad news before, but this was somehow more personal.

"Let's make the drinks," Jack suggested. "I get the feeling we're going to need them."

Five minutes later they sat at the table and Bobby fixed his attention on Olaf.

"So spill. Why have you gone to the trouble of finding me?"

"Your brother, Keith, asked me to find you."

"Not my dad?" The hurt and disappointment was obvious.

"I'm sorry," Olaf said gently, "but your dad died a few weeks ago."

Bobby swallowed hard. "God, he didn't tell me."

Olaf thought that was odd, but Bobby continued.

"Even after all this time, I hoped, I prayed he wanted to see me again."

"There's no easy way to say this, Bobby—"

"Call me Rob. I'm Rob Armstrong now. I haven't been Bobby Sargent since the day I left."

"Rob," Olaf acknowledged. "Keith didn't know if you were alive or dead. He asked me to investigate. He just wanted to know what had happened to his brother after all this time."

"He never forgot me?"

For a moment, Olaf could hear the teenage boy he'd been.

"He never forgot you."

"I never forgot him either. My annoying little brother." Rob gave a fond smile.

"Not so little now," Olaf said. "He's got a wife and teenage kids."

"Tell him the rest," Paul murmured.

Rob frowned. "The rest of what?"

Olaf took a deep breath. "Keith didn't know if your dad had killed you. That was the rumour."

Rob's jaw dropped. "People thought Dad had murdered me?"

"Yeah. He lived with that suspicion until the day he died. Keith thought it was true."

"I thought Dad might kill me," Rob admitted. "He was so angry with me. That's why I ran."

"You vanished because you thought he was going to kill you?" Olaf asked.

Rob nodded. "Yeah. I couldn't tell the cops. You know he was one?"

"Yeah."

"I hate the fucking cops," Rob said.

That was definitely Bobby talking.

Olaf couldn't help the lip twitch which Rob obviously spotted.

"What? Don't tell me you're cops."

"Cop." Paul pointed to himself. "Ex-cop." He pointed at Olaf.

Rob groaned, but to Olaf's surprise, Jack chuckled.

"I told you you've got to move on. They're not all like your dad."

They all chuckled at Rob's disgusted grunt.

"You'd get on well with my mum," Paul said. "She hates the cops too."

"And yet you joined the police force," Jack said.

Paul shrugged. "Someone had to."

"What happened that night, Bobby—Rob?" Paul asked.

Rob ran his fingers through his hair. "You know, it's so long ago I barely remember."

But Olaf knew he was lying. That night would be forever etched in Rob's mind.

"You got caught with an older guy," Olaf said.

To his surprise, Rob smirked. "I did. I finally managed to hook the guy after months of trying, and my dad walked in on us. He was furious. He got Jacob arrested and I went ballistic."

"You were below the age of consent," Paul pointed out.

Rob shot him an angry look. "He was twenty-one. I was sixteen. Only five years."

Olaf was damned sure from the storm brewing in Paul's eyes that his lover disagreed with that perspective, as did he, but it was a long time ago. That wasn't what they were here for, and there was double that age gap between him and Paul. He sought to change the subject. "So you had a fight with your dad?"

"Yeah. A real knock-out screaming match. Dad hit me as usual, but this time I was so angry I punched him back and gave him a black eye. Surprised the hell out of both of us, I can tell you. But I knew straight away it wasn't safe for me to stay. My dad would never forgive me for hitting him. I had to get off the island."

"You were only sixteen. A minor," Paul said. "How did you get away?"

Rob hesitated. "Someone helped me. A friend. He had a boat. He took me to the mainland and found me a hotel to stay in. Then he found me a place to stay with friends while we worked out what to do next."

"A friend?" Olaf asked.

"Yeah. An adult. No, not like that," Rob snapped, obviously gauging their expressions. "He was a friend of the family who knew what Dad was like. If Dad had cared at all, I'd have come back. But he didn't so I stayed in Portsmouth for a bit, then I found a job in Southampton. I lived there for ten years."

Olaf sat up straight, suddenly connecting the dots. "John Parkin. He's the friend of the family."

So all that bluster about hating Bobby had been

just that. Bluster and hot air to divert Olaf's attention. And it had worked.

Rob looked surprised. "You've met him? Yes, it was John. He was great to me."

"Was? Or is? You're still in contact, aren't you?"

"You know Bobby might not want to be found."

That was what had bothered Olaf. Like Parkin still knew Bobby. If Olaf hadn't been distracted with Paul, he might have worked it out sooner.

"Sometimes." Rob frowned. "He didn't tell me about you or my dad though."

Olaf would buy Parkin a pint for keeping quiet.

"You never..." Olaf let it hang.

"God no. No." Rob looked revolted. "He was like a father to me. Better than my real dad. Besides, I was in love."

"Who with?" Paul asked.

"Me," Jack said.

And another piece fell into place. "Jacob. Jack. You weren't charged."

"No. They kept me for forty-eight hours then escorted me off the island in case I corrupted any more minors. Sargent's reputation was in the toilet by that time. They didn't want the spotlight on him or them." Jack grimaced. "I know I was really lucky. Other men weren't, as the cops kept telling me."

"Parkin knew how we felt about each other. He made Jack promise to keep his hands off me. He was very forceful." At Jack's snort, Rob grinned. "What John didn't know..."

"So you've been together ever since?" Olaf asked.

Rob smiled at Jack. "He's my soulmate."

Olaf felt Paul's hand cling briefly to his.

"What about Tony Dobson?"

Rob looked startled. "I haven't thought about him since the day I left."

I guess that answers that one. Olaf felt rather sorry for Dobson.

"What's he up to?" Rob asked.

"He's married with kids."

"Good for him. It would be nice to meet him and his husband."

"He married a woman," Olaf said.

Rob frowned. "But he was gay."

"He thought you were dead. He was scared it would happen to him," Olaf said. "Tony's father saw your dad carrying a rug out of the house in the middle of the night after the fight."

"What?" Rob looked flabbergasted. "What the hell? I was already gone by then."

"Dobson's father was convinced he was taking you to his boat to dump your body out to sea."

"Dad probably dumped the rug because there was my blood on it," Rob said. "So Dobson didn't investigate?"

"It doesn't look like it."

"Typical. Old man Dobson hated me." He paused, then his grin was pure Bobby Sargent. "All the parents hated me. I was always getting their precious sons into trouble."

"I heard about your reputation," Olaf said.

"I was a pain in the arse," Rob agreed. "I was so scared that I was always fighting, you know?"

"Scared of your dad?"

"Mainly of being outed. I guess I thought if I behaved like an arsehole they'd never believe I was a poof. It was a toxic way to live. Then I met Jacob Armstrong." His smile turned soft as he looked at Jack. "Suddenly there was this openly gay man who didn't give a shit what people thought about him. I wanted to be like him, you know?"

Olaf nodded. He did know. If it hadn't been for Paul...

Rob gave a chuckle. "Jacob didn't notice me at first."

"I noticed you," Jack contradicted, "but I also knew how old you were. Jailbait."

"Eventually I wore him down."

"Only to have your dad catch you fucking?"

Rob shook his head. "We were kissing, that's all. Jacob refused to fuck me until I was much older."

Olaf blinked. "Wait, Sargent had you arrested for *kissing* Rob?"

Jacob grimaced. "Yeah, he told them I was a nonce. You can imagine how they treated me. Except Rob vanished and there was a really uneasy atmosphere in the nick. I didn't understand why. But suddenly I was being hustled out of the police station and made to get off the island pronto. They wouldn't tell me anything except the usual threats."

"How did you two meet up again?" Paul asked.

"Rob tracked down my parents. I'd gone back there."

"I knew his parents lived just outside Portsmouth. I rang every Armstrong in the phone book until I found the right one."

"You were persistent." Paul looked impressed.

"I loved him," Rob said simply.

"I couldn't believe it when he turned up on the doorstep," Jack admitted. "At first I tried to tell him to go away. I didn't want to get arrested again. But he wouldn't go. And then my mum came home, and she found out the truth about why I'd come home early. She wasn't impressed. I thought she was going to throw me out."

"But we convinced her that Jacob had only kissed me, and I told her I was very persistent. And that I loved him, and I wanted to spend the rest of my life with him."

"And she believed you," Paul asked, obviously sceptical. "You were sixteen."

"Seventeen by then and yes, she believed me. But she laid down ground rules. No sex, no living together until I was twenty-one, I had to go to university, and no firm commitments until I graduated."

"And how did the rules work out?" Paul asked.

Rob and Jack looked at each other, then looked away. Olaf guessed that was the answer.

"I finished my A-levels and went to university to study law," Rob said.

"I finished my degree, then moved in with Rob," Jack said. "My parents calmed down once they understood we were serious about each other."

"I'm amazed you're still together," Olaf admitted. At sixteen, and even at twenty-one, he'd barely known how to scratch his ass.

"When I went to uni, Jack told me he was dumping me so that I could screw around and have fun," Rob admitted. "He never wanted me to feel resentful about what I didn't have."

"What happened?" Paul asked.

Rob looked haunted for a moment. "I did as he said. Screwed any man with a pulse whether it was legal or not. Then I went to Jack on my knees and begged him to take me back because all I wanted was him."

"Wow." Paul sounded impressed.

"I said no. And no. And no." Jack huffed but it was obvious how much he loved Rob. "Have you ever met anyone you can't say no to?"

"Yes," Olaf murmured, deliberately not looking at Paul.

Rob grinned as he looked between the two of them. "You have to go after what you want. Right?"

"But what if you want more than one thing?" Paul asked.

"Then you have to decide what you can't live without. In my case, I'd have given up uni and the other guys, to be with Jack. He didn't ask me to do that, but I would have."

"I gave up the job of my dreams in London to be with Rob," Jack said. "My life was empty without him."

Olaf thought it was time they changed the subject. This was getting too near the knuckle for both of them. "Look, Rob, there's a couple of things I need to tell you. There's a reason your dad didn't contact you."

"Because he hated me being gay."

Olaf shook his head. "He hired a private detective to search for you."

"He did?" Rob looked confused. "But they didn't find me?"

"They did and that's how we found you. But Stuart Reynolds decided to withhold the information. He didn't trust your father. I'm sorry."

The conflict was clear on Rob's face. "All this time I thought Dad didn't give a shit about me." He sighed. "Stuart Reynolds? I remember that name."

"He lived near you," Olaf said. "He knew what your dad was like."

Rob nodded. "He was probably right, although it helps to know Dad did try to find me. What's the other thing?"

"I need to tell your brother that you're alive and well," Olaf said, "but I don't have to give him your address if you don't want me to."

Rob sucked in a breath. "It's overwhelming, you know?"

Olaf tore a page out of his notebook. "This is Keith's number. If you want to call him."

Rob stared at the piece of paper as if it were a live snake. "I want to talk to him, but I'm scared, too. What if he never forgives me?"

"You've got a lot of ground to cover," Olaf said. "But he's made the first move. Now it's up to you."

Jack wrapped his arm around Rob's shoulders. "I'll be with you every step of the way."

Olaf looked away, fiercely aching for that kind

of commitment.

They said goodbye and returned to the car.

Paul let out an explosive breath as soon as both doors shut. "That was...I don't know what that was."

"The end of my first case," Olaf said. "I found the missing boy."

Paul grinned at him. "You're always so practical. But first you have to call your client."

Olaf grimaced. "I should be happy, but I'm just nervous."

"Why? You solved the case. He said up front that it didn't matter if his brother never wanted to meet. He just needed to know whether he was alive or dead."

Olaf looked at Paul. "Okay then. Let's make the call."

He pressed the number. The phone rang and rang, and he was about to give up when it was suddenly answered.

"Hello." The voice sounded breathless. "Who is it?"

"Keith, it's Olaf Skandik."

"Oh, hi. Sorry, I was at the end of the garden. I'm sorry, I haven't had time to go through Dad's papers yet."

"It's okay, you don't have to," Olaf said, "I've got news for you."

There was a long silence. "Yes?"

Olaf had never heard one word so full of hope and fear.

"I've just met your brother."

Chapter 14

Wednesday

There was a thump, as if Keith had dropped the phone, then the silence stretched so long, Olaf wasn't sure if they were still connected.

"Keith? Keith? Are you all right?"

Then a brusque female voice said, "Who's this?"

"Olaf Skandik. Is that Miriam?"

"Yes. What have you said to Keith? He's crying. Oh God, is it bad news?" Miriam sounded frantic.

"I hope not. I've just met Bobby."

"Oh my God. Really? He's not dead?"

Unseen by her, Olaf grinned. "He wasn't five minutes ago."

"Is he all right? Is he—?"

"Give me the phone, you daft cow."

Olaf grinned as he heard Keith's muffled voice.

"Olaf, are you still there?"

"I am," Olaf assured him.

"Sorry about that. It was just the shock. Is Bobby all right?"

"Rob is fine and happy. He's just as shocked as you are. Listen, I'll send you a report when I get home. We did as you asked and left your phone number with him. I think he might need a little time to process."

"Is he still...?"

"Gay? Yes, he's still gay."

Olaf grinned as he saw Paul roll his eyes. "He's married to a lovely guy."

There was no way he was going to spoil Rob's surprise.

"How much can you tell me?" Keith asked.

Olaf thought about it for a moment. "He left because he thought your dad would kill him."

"I thought so. But where did he go?"

"He had help," Olaf said in a non-committal tone. "I think Rob should tell you his story."

"What if he doesn't call?"

"He will, Keith. He's just as shocked as you are, but he wants his little brother back."

There was a pause, then a choked, "Gotta go." And he was gone.

Olaf understood. Keith needed to cry again.

He turned to Paul. "Do you think your mum would make me a coffee if I asked nicely? I really need to decompress before the drive home."

"Damn it, I wish I could drive." Paul cursed. "Let me call her. We could stay in my flat tonight if you want."

"What do you want to do?"

"Go home," Paul admitted.

Olaf understood that he didn't mean the flat. "Do you want to pick up fresh clothes?"

"Yeah, good idea. Hey, Mum, it's Paul. Yes, I know you know it's me. Listen, Olaf's just wrapped up his first case. He needs a cuppa before we drive home. We're close by. Could we come to you? Great, thanks. Don't forget...I don't think you're old. Well, not *that* old."

"Mattie's going to kill you," Olaf said as Paul disconnected the call.

"She loves me," Paul said confidently.

"That's not what she says." Olaf grinned at Paul's snort.

It took thirty minutes to reach Mattie and Jim's place, and by the time they arrived, Olaf's nerves were stretched as tight as a drum. He knew why; it just wasn't in his power to solve.

"Are you worried Rob won't phone Keith?" Paul asked as he undid his seatbelt.

Olaf thought about lying but this was Paul, and he would always know. "No. I'm sure Rob will call him. Yeah, he needs time to process, but you saw him. He was thrilled Keith tried to find him."

"Then what's the problem?"

Olaf turned to look at Paul. "I'm worried you'll want to stay here."

Paul sighed and reached up to kiss Olaf. "It's got to happen sometime, babe."

"I know," Olaf said morosely.

"Let's go in before Mum gets annoyed."

Olaf knew Paul was deflecting, but he was the one who'd asked to come here. Now was not the time to argue with Paul.

Olaf found himself on the end of a Mattie Owens hug the second he walked in the door.

"Put him down, Mum," Paul ordered. "You don't know where he's been."

"Thanks," Olaf said over Mattie's head.

Paul smirked at him. "You're welcome."

Mattie stepped back and fixed Olaf with a stare that would have been frightening if Paul didn't have the exact same expression. "You found him? You found Bobby?"

Olaf took her hands. "I can't give you the details, but yes, we found him, and he's happy."

"Thank God for that," she said. "Jim and I...we've been so worried. But everybody lives. You know he was Jim's friend?"

"He said he used to play in Rose's garden."

"We all did," Jim said. "I wasn't as close to him as Danny. I was older than them. But they liked coming to Mum's place to get away from their parents. Rose made it her mission to collect waifs and strays."

Olaf nodded. He'd met Daniel Gillard's homophobic mother. He'd also been adopted by Rose, yet another waif and stray.

"The tea's made and the coffee is brewing, Olaf."

The Owenses were hard-core tea drinkers, but Mattie had purchased a coffee machine when Liam joined the family.

"Does Keith know?" Jim asked.

"Yes. It's up to Rob now if he wants to call Keith."

Of course, Mattie was on the name change in a flash. "Rob, not Bobby?"

Olaf nodded.

"Don't question the lad," Jim scolded. "You know he can't talk about the case."

Mattie pouted but she didn't question him any further. Olaf bent to kiss her cheek.

"If I get permission, I'll tell you more," he promised.

She patted his cheek. "You're a good lad."

"Watch her," Paul warned. "You know she'll try to wiggle it out of you."

Mattie poked her tongue out.

Jim sighed, but Paul and Mattie smirked at each other. Olaf thought how many times he'd counted to ten, and then again, in the early days of their relationship. Jim must also be an expert in several languages by now. One day he'd have to ask him.

Olaf relaxed as Paul, Jim, and Mattie sat around the kitchen table and talked about the family. He didn't really listen to the conversation, lost in his own thoughts. This had been an intense case but satisfying to be reuniting—he hoped—a family. He realised how lucky he was. His parents loved him and only wanted the best for him, even if his best and their best weren't the same thing.

"Olaf?" Paul leaned forwards and placed a hand on his. "Is everything okay?"

Olaf clasped Paul's hand between his. "I just realised how lucky I am with my parents."

Paul blinked. "Uh...if you say so."

The relationship between Paul and Olaf's parents was cordial, friendly even, but Olaf's mom had found it hard to hide the fact she wished Paul had been a woman. Olaf knew a lot of the issue was wrapped up in her desire to be a grandmother to Olaf's children.

"They didn't throw me out when they found out I was gay," Olaf said.

Paul scowled. "No, they just shoved you back in

the closet and turned the key."

"I did that to myself."

On one of his visits to the UK when he and Paul were on one of their 'on' moments, Olaf had shared a bottle of fine brandy with Jim while he waited for Paul to finish his shift. Jim had confessed he'd always been worried that Paul would never find the love of his life because he could never commit to anyone. Olaf had told him that Paul was the only person he'd ever met who demanded Olaf step out of the closet and find his happiness. They were opposites in every way, but they'd been exactly what each other needed.

He could have ended up like Tony Dobson, too scared to take what he wanted. He shivered.

"No more dark thoughts," Paul demanded.

Olaf smiled at him. "No more dark thoughts."

By the time they left Mattie and Jim's, Paul was looking as exhausted as Olaf felt, and leaning against Olaf for support.

"Let's stay at your flat tonight and go back in the morning," Olaf suggested as they walked to their car.

"Thank God." Paul almost moaned. "I don't think I could face a long journey now."

"You should have said."

"I didn't want to disappoint you. I know you don't like the flat."

"You never disappoint me," Olaf assured Paul. He ignored the second part.

Paul dimpled at him. "You know that's not true."

Olaf kissed the top of his head. "You're perfect for me."

"You're feeling insecure, aren't you?" Paul said.

"You're very perceptive."

"Who is bothering you the most? Keith or Bobby?"

"Neither of them," Olaf admitted.

"Then what's the problem?"

"It's Tony Dobson. It's like he's the forgotten man in all this. He loved Bobby and kept that secret for decades. He was so scared and made a bad decision. Now we find Bobby's been happily married all along. You heard him. He didn't even remember Dobson."

"Maybe he didn't know Dobson had feelings for him," Paul suggested.

"I bet you he did, and he loved it."

"Give him a break," Paul said. "He was sixteen years old and thinking with his dick. I remember what I was like then. I loved it when girls, and boys, fancied me."

"Nothing much has changed there," Olaf said.

Paul shoved him, then yelped. "For fuck's sake." He clutched onto his arm. "When will this be over?"

"You could try not shoving me."

Olaf grinned at Paul's disgusted expression. Still, Paul had a point. Olaf was projecting adult values on a kid who had barely known what life was.

They were in the car before Paul spoke again. "You're still uneasy, aren't you?"

"I think there's going to be a lot of fallout from

this case," Olaf mused.

"Stuart Reynolds knew Bobby was alive and living in Southampton," Paul said. "The report from Reynolds proves that. But he never told Robert or Keith."

"All those years he could have stopped the suspicion. Fuck, Parkin could have said something at any point. Why didn't either of them speak?" Suddenly angry, Olaf punched the steering wheel. "Sargent tanked his career, and his other son suspected him of murder. I don't get it."

"He would rather have been suspected of murder than have a gay son."

"And Bobby—Rob—is just as bad," Olaf continued. "Why did he never contact Keith? One Facebook message. A comment via Parkin. It was his fucking brother. All those secrets and lies."

"Maybe John Parkin just wanted to keep the peace. He knew Bobby was all right. He knew Robert had calmed down once Bobby left. You know what Keith said. He was easier to live with."

Olaf grunted. Miriam Sargent might say different.

"Let's go home. We can watch the footie, eat pizza, and drink beer in bed."

"You know that sounds like heaven," Olaf agreed.

"And have sex," Paul added.

"Of course."

That was a given.

Thursday

Well, sex would have been a given if they

hadn't crashed out before the first half of the soccer game had finished. Not surprisingly, Paul was asleep first, resting his cheek on Olaf's chest. Olaf made it to the second half, but Paul was warm, the match uninspiring, and his lids grew heavy. He fell asleep to the sound of cheers, but he couldn't be bothered to wake up and find out which team had scored.

When he woke, however, it was a different matter. The space beside him was empty, but the mattress dipped, and his cock was hard enough to drill nails. Olaf raised his head to see Paul between his legs.

"What are you doing?"

Paul pulled off Olaf's cock with a noisy slurp. "If you need to ask that, I'm doing something wrong, lover."

In hindsight, it *had* been a stupid question, but Olaf had just opened his eyes.

"You could carry on while I wake up," Olaf suggested.

Paul tapped his chin. "Hmmm, I don't know. You didn't seem that enthusiastic before."

Olaf nudged the tip of his hard dick against Paul's glistening lips. "I'm enthusiastic. Really I am. And your mouth felt so good." Olaf wasn't above begging if it would get him what he wanted. Which was Paul's hot mouth around the length of him.

Paul licked the head of Olaf's cock with his slick tongue.

Olaf whimpered. "You feel so good."

Paul's mouth was all over him, nibbling down

the shaft, tormenting him with his lips and tongue and more than a grazing of teeth, just the way he liked.

Olaf clutched Paul's head, his fingers sinking into the soft strands of hair. He tried to guide Paul's mouth, but Paul wasn't having any of it.

He pulled off again to snap, "My rodeo, cowboy."

Olaf groaned and lay back. He didn't care as long as Paul didn't stop what he was doing. Paul cupped his sac, rolling the orbs, as he sucked the tip of Olaf's cock. Olaf's attention zeroed down to his cock and balls, his orgasm coiling, not there yet, but waiting for just the right moment.

He looked at the concentration on Paul's face as he focused on Olaf's dick. Paul had one job and he was the man to do it. Paul sank until he nosed the patch of short hair around Olaf's cock. Olaf was taken into deep, wet heat. He shouted in pleasure.

"Neighbours," Paul said.

A reminder that the walls were paper-thin.

"Fuck. The. Neighbours," Olaf said succinctly.

Paul chuckled. "Not my type." Then, to Olaf's relief, he smoothed a hand over Olaf's belly and went back to the job at hand.

Olaf closed his eyes and let his focus narrow down again to the pleasure Paul's mouth gave him. He wanted to hold Paul's head in the perfect place, fuck Paul's mouth, bury his cock down Paul's throat. But this was all Paul's show, and he would lick and suck and nibble and bite until the climax building in Olaf's balls exploded.

As if the thought of climaxing gave him permission, Olaf yelled again as his balls emptied in frantic spurts through his rigid-as-fuck cock. Paul took everything Olaf gave him and swallowed it down. Olaf arched his back before crashing back down to the bed, every muscle suddenly lax. Paul rested his cheek on Olaf's thigh as they both recovered their breath.

"You?" Olaf finally managed.

"Hold me?"

Olaf held out his arms and Paul wriggled into them, sighing happily when Paul's arms closed around him.

"I needed this," Paul admitted.

I'm never going to let you go. But Olaf couldn't say it out loud, scared that his highly-strung partner would take that moment to run away. Olaf ran his hands down the smooth skin of Paul's back to cup his ass. Paul's hard dick prodded Olaf's belly, reminding him he had a job to do.

"Use your hand on me?" Paul begged.

Olaf engulfed Paul's dick in his hand. Paul sighed and pushed in closer. Olaf jacked him slowly, loving the way Paul started to babble a stream of incoherency into the crook of Olaf's neck as he got closer to his climax. It didn't take long. Paul was already too much on the edge to wait. He came with a choked-off cry, spurting over Olaf's fingers and onto his belly.

Finally, Paul sighed and pressed a kiss against Olaf's collar bone. "I needed that too."

"The blow job, the cuddle, or the hand job?" Olaf queried.

"Any. All. I could stay like this forever."

"Let's go home and cuddle in our bed."

Paul seemed to sigh in agreement. "Could we teleport there?"

"'Fraid not, sweetheart. We need to clean up before we leave. And you need to pack extra clothes."

"You take a shower, and I'll make breakfast," Paul suggested.

Olaf furrowed his brow. "What have we got to eat?" Mattie had cleared out the contents of Paul's fridge for him when Paul decided to spend his sick leave with Olaf.

"Last night's pizza."

"Okay, fair enough."

But neither of them moved. Olaf was in no hurry. He'd solved his case, and unless Liam called telling him different, he had no other work. At the moment, holding Paul was far more important.

Olaf came out of the shower to discover Paul in the bedroom, eating leftover pizza and rummaging through his drawers for fresh clothes he could manage to wear.

"I hope you left a slice for me," Olaf grumbled.

"Nope. Ate it all," Paul said cheerfully. He rolled his eyes at Olaf's glower. "'Course I left you some. I'm not that stupid. I know what you get like when you're hangry."

Olaf grunted and went in search of pizza. He didn't get hangry. Maybe a little grumpy when he was hungry. Which he had to admit, if only to himself, was the definition of hangry.

He returned to the bedroom with a slice in either hand. He offered one to Paul who shook his head. "All yours, babe. I'm going to take a shower. By the way, Sam might meet us on the ferry. He wants to cadge a lift home because Liam is busy. He spent the night in Portsmouth so he's coming home early."

Olaf lifted one eyebrow. "He trusted himself to stay away from Liam for the night?"

"I know. Progress, right?"

They both knew how momentous it was. Even when Liam was so obviously recovered from his breakdown, Sam had been scared to leave him alone. Just in case.

"Also, Liam called me to beg a lift for Sam."

Olaf snorted. They both had co-dependency issues.

The journey to the ferry was smooth, only a brief delay around Guildford hindering their path. Paul slept for part of the journey, but he was awake by the time they reached the terminal in Portsmouth. They bickered for a few minutes about who was going to get the drinks, but as Paul had only one working hand, it was obvious who was going to lose the argument.

Olaf spotted Sam on the ferry, looking out of one of the salt-covered windows. He pointed to Paul who headed over to see his brother.

"You look like shite," Paul said abruptly.

It was blunt but accurate. Sam was pale and he had huge dark smudges under his eyes.

"Thanks." Sam sighed. "Way to make me feel good."

"You're overworking."

"You've been talking to Liam," Sam said sourly.

"I've got eyes. When was the last time you slept?" When Sam hesitated, he nodded. "Get an assistant, idiot. And don't give me that crap about not being able to afford it. I spoke to Liam."

"Traitor," Sam muttered.

Olaf wasn't sure if Sam was talking about his brother or his husband. Probably both.

As Olaf drove off the ferry, his phone beeped.

"Could you check the phone?" he asked Paul. He was nervous about missing potential business.

Paul picked it up and grinned. "It's a message from Keith."

"What does it say?" Olaf asked.

"He called."

"Who called?" Sam asked sleepily from the backseat.

"Rob Armstrong," Paul said.

Olaf breathed easier. *Now* his first job was complete.

Chapter 15

Friday

Olaf spent the following morning in the office, writing up the final report for Keith and adding up the expenses. Liam was at home, fussing over Sam. Olaf had a feeling Liam was ready to lay down the law unless Sam agreed to employ an assistant. Or tie him to the bed. Liam wasn't fussy. Liam had confided in Olaf that one of Sam's cousins was looking for work after finishing her degree. Liam had already employed her. Now he just had to get Sam to agree.

Olaf breathed a sigh of relief once the report was finished. He sent it to Keith then shut down the laptop. It was time he went and found his boy. He was going to join Paul for lunch and every other time he could make it, because soon Paul would be returning to work, even if it was only desk duty, and Olaf would be alone once more. He was dreading that moment more than he'd admit. Paul had initially fussed at Olaf's proposal, but he admitted he would have found an excuse to visit Olaf at the office.

But the house was empty and there was no smell of coffee or soup. There wasn't even a note propped up on the kitchen table, their usual method of communication. Come to think of it, he'd messaged Paul earlier in the day but hadn't received a reply. That only happened when he was working. Oh well, maybe Paul had finally gone to see Logan again. He headed for the coffee pot but before he got there, his phone buzzed.

"Hey, Olaf," Nick greeted him. "What's up with your boy?"

Olaf froze, coffee cup in hand. "What do you mean?"

So, not at Logan's then.

"He's walking the cliffs at Compton Chine," Nick said.

"He's what?"

Olaf had put down the cup and was hunting for his keys before he'd finished the sentence. Paul must be really upset. He never walked if he could possibly help it. It was a waste of good fucking time, as he once put it.

"We've just driven past him. Do you want us to turn back?"

"No," Olaf said, "it's okay, I'm on my way."

Thankfully he was at home and not at the office. Freshwater wasn't that far from Compton Chine.

"Okay. Catch you guys tomorrow at Jeff's?"

"Yeah," Olaf said absently. He'd forgotten they'd arranged a boys' night with Jeff cooking and Cam 'supervising'. "We'll be there."

He disconnected the call and ran out of the door, heading straight for the car. How the hell had Paul gotten to Compton Chine? Did he actually take a bus? He just hoped he got there before Paul decided to go somewhere else.

To his relief, Paul was exactly where Nick had said he was, staring out over the waves, his hands in his pockets and his expression sombre. He didn't look surprised when Olaf joined him.

Olaf wrapped Paul in his arms and kissed the top of his head. "Are you going to tell me what's wrong, sweetheart?"

Paul sighed and sunk into Olaf's embrace. "How did you find me?"

"Nick and Logan saw you as they drove past. They called me. How did you get here?"

"Liam dropped me here. He said he'd pick me up if I called him. I needed to think, and the house was closing in on me."

Olaf stroked Paul's hair. "Are you done thinking, or do you need me to go away?" He would leave Paul here if that's what he wanted, but Paul buried closer against him.

"I'm done."

"Then talk to me, sweetheart."

"I turned down the job move," Paul said.

A knot of tension Olaf hadn't even known was there eased at Paul's words. "Thank you." He couldn't even pretend he was sorry that Paul didn't want to work in the abused and trafficked children's unit.

"I made that decision weeks ago," Paul said. "I just didn't want to admit it to myself."

Olaf kissed him again, knowing how hard that must have been for his ambitious boyfriend. "Maybe another chance of promotion will come up."

Paul's sigh was almost painful. "I don't think so."

"They won't offer you another promotion?" Olaf asked indignantly. "That's ridiculous. You'd be an asset wherever you went."

"That's sweet of you, lover." Paul raised his head, and his smile was tender. "But I phoned the guv five minutes before you arrived and handed in my resignation."

Olaf froze. "You did?"

"I did."

"But why?"

"Because Jack was right. I had to decide what I couldn't live without. And that was you."

"Me?" Olaf had a hard time forcing the word out.

"Yes, you." Now Paul sounded almost amused.

"But your career. Your ambition. This is everything you've ever wanted."

"It was. But times change. *I've* changed. I've spent all our relationship insisting things had to go my way."

"I did that too," Olaf protested.

Paul tilted his head to look at him. "You gave up your job and family and travelled halfway across the world to live with me."

"But I gained a new family and became an out gay man for the first time in my life. And we still lived apart."

"Exactly. And I don't want that anymore. I want to share your bed every night. Wake to morning breath and blowjobs. Watch your football which I don't understand and eat because you insist on three meals a day and—"

Olaf placed a finger over his mouth. "I get it, sweetheart. I get it. I'm the adventure you want."

Paul frowned. "Yes, that's it exactly. Where did you get that phrase from?"

"It was from one of Sam's gay romance books. And you were the adventure I wanted so I moved here. And now you realise I'm your adventure too. But what are you going to do? Are you applying to the island force?"

"Hell no. I've got to work out my notice, but then I'm going to become your partner."

Olaf's jaw dropped open. "What?"

Paul beamed at him. "Owens and Skandik, private dicks."

"Skandik and Owens," Olaf corrected before his brain had time to send up the red flags.

What was he thinking? He and Paul could never work together. They'd kill each other. Olaf was methodical and steady. Paul was...well, according to his co-workers, Paul was like that too, only not many people got to see that side of Paul.

Paul gave him a sweet yet very smug smile. "We'll have all the time in the world to discuss it."

"No, it's a dreadful idea. No. Just no," Owen reiterated.

"You don't want to work with me?"

Olaf rolled his eyes as Paul jutted out his lip. "Don't pout. I just don't think there's enough work for the two of us."

"You don't know that."

"No, I don't. But we worked out our finances on me starting a business. Not both of us. What if I don't get another case?"

"What if you do and you need help?" Paul argued. "I've spoken to Sam, and he thinks we can swing it."

"And when were you going to tell me you spoke to my accountant?"

"Our accountant," Paul corrected. "And he's my big brother. Of course I spoke to him."

Olaf couldn't really argue with that.

"Let's go back to the office. We need to make plans," Paul suggested.

"Do I get a choice in this?" Olaf asked.

Paul gave him a withering look. "Don't be ridiculous."

Olaf really should have run away when he first met the gobby Brit. He really should.

The office looked even smaller with the two of them in it.

"We're going to have to get a bigger office," Paul mused. "If we're both here and so is Liam, there's not enough room to swing a cat."

"No cat swinging," Olaf said hastily. "Definitely no cat swinging. And we can't afford to get a bigger office, otherwise I'd have taken the room next door too."

Nibs had offered him a great deal to take both rooms on the floor, but Olaf had been worried he wouldn't be able to pay the rent.

"Leave it with me," Paul said confidently.

"Have you won the lotto or something?" Olaf asked.

"I wish." Paul reached up and kissed Olaf's

cheek.

Oh, what the hell. If it all went wrong, Olaf would do the one thing he said he'd never do and beg his parents for help. They'd be so shocked they might just say yes.

"Okay then." Olaf grinned at Paul. "Skandik and Owens, private detectives. Here to find the lost, the missing, and the cheating husbands."

"Now that's more like it. High five."

As they high fived each other, the office door opened. Olaf and Paul turned to face the man standing on the doorstep. Olaf's first impression was that he was hot. As in stunningly beautiful model gorgeous hot. He was almost Olaf's height, with jet black hair, eyes so dark they looked almost black, and cheekbones to kill for. Paul had noticed it too, of course. He could tell by the speculative look in Paul's eyes.

The man looked confused. "Mr Skandik?"

"That's me," Olaf said, "Can I help you?"

"Uh, my name is Jace Comerford. We had an appointment at three."

Olaf had completely forgotten about the appointment Liam had made for him. So much had happened since then.

"Oh right, I'm sorry, Mr Comerford. Come in." Then Olaf looked at the space and Liam's books piled up in the corner. "No, wait, let's go down to the Lagoon. We're in the middle of changing things here."

Paul held out his hand. "I'm Paul Owens, Olaf's business partner."

"Oh, I didn't realise." Comerford shook Paul's

hand and then Olaf's.

Olaf led the way down the stairs. Fortunately, the Lagoon wasn't that busy and they found a quiet corner. Wig, with unusual tact, took their order and left them alone. Comerford seemed lost in his own thoughts.

Once they all had drinks in front of them, Olaf said, "How may we help you, Mr Comerford?"

"I'm Jace Comerford, of Comerford Industries."

It meant nothing to Olaf, but Paul nodded. "You're based in Portsmouth."

"That's right."

"So why do you need our help?"

Comerford huffed out a breath. "You were recommended by David Reynolds."

Why would Reynolds do...oh! So this was how it would work. Reynolds would pass on jobs he didn't necessarily want to handle.

"You're gay, Mr Comerford?" Olaf asked, his tone cautious.

"Jace, please. And yes, I'm gay, and no, it's not a secret," he said bluntly. "No one is blackmailing me."

"So what can we do to help you?"

Jace looked up, the pain naked on his face. "I need you to find my lying, cheating, sack of shit husband."

Epilogue

It took weeks for Bobby—now Rob—and Keith to talk through the thirty-five years and their differences, to get to the point where they felt ready to meet. Keith had kept in contact with Olaf, and he'd admitted that he felt a lot more anger towards his brother for not returning than he'd expected. It had taken a while to work through that.

They finally agreed to meet at the end of September. Rob and Jack would travel to the island and stay in an Airbnb. Keith wasn't ready to have them stay with his family. He asked Olaf to join him at Ryde terminal to give him moral support.

It just so happened Paul was also off that weekend, so he met them from the earlier cat. He was still working out his notice period. Olaf missed him like hell, and their Skype sessions had become more awkward than sexy as they waited for Paul's final day in the force.

"Fuck, I'm nervous," Keith muttered as they waited for the catamaran. He scuffed his feet. "Fuckin' ridiculous."

Olaf looked at him. "You're just about to meet your brother for the first time in thirty-five years.

It's not ridiculous."

"I'm desperate to see him, but I'm still so angry, you know?"

Paul leaned past Olaf and patted his arm. "Of course you are. Don't hide that. Rob could have come back at any time or got in contact with you. He's got serious making up to do. But don't let your anger ruin your future relationship."

Keith nodded and sucked in a deep breath. He smiled gratefully at Paul. "Logan said it will take time."

It amused Olaf how protective Paul was with Keith. Paul knew Keith needed gentle handling. Paul had introduced Keith to Logan, and Miriam had thanked Paul over and over for seeing past the angry man to the vulnerable boy who never got past losing his brother. Olaf pointed out to Paul that they weren't meant to get emotionally involved with their clients. Paul flipped him off. Life as normal.

"There's the cat," Olaf murmured.

"Shit. Shit." Keith looked as if he wanted to bolt.

"Take a deep breath," Paul ordered. "Rob is going to be as nervous as you."

"I can't think of him as Rob. He'll always be Bobby to me."

People started pouring off the catamaran. Olaf looked for the tall man with short-cropped white hair. He spotted him with Jack.

"That's him," he said to Keith, who rocked back on his heels.

"Oh my God. He's the living spit of my Dad."

Keith started to laugh. "I wish Dad could have seen him."

Olaf saw the moment Rob spotted Keith. His hand went over his mouth and even from here it was obvious he was on the verge of tears.

"I don't know what to do," Keith said, his voice raw.

Paul rolled his eyes. "Go over there and hug him senseless. You can punch him later."

Before he'd finished, Keith was on the move. Rob met him in the middle. There was a painful moment of staring, then they hugged. Not the awkward guy hug, but wrapped around each other and sobbing on each other's shoulders.

"Maybe we should have done this in private," Paul said.

Olaf agreed. He was going to be in tears in a moment.

Jack skirted around the brothers to join them, his eyes gleaming suspiciously. He shook Olaf's and Paul's hands. "Rob has been so nervous about this. He wasn't sure how Keith would greet him."

"The violence might come later," Paul muttered.

Jack sighed. "Rob's ready for it. There's a lot to make up for."

"We'll make sure Keith is okay and leave you guys to it," Olaf said. "This is for family."

"Thank you for finding us," Jack said. "Rob's had my family, but it's not the same."

"No, it's not," Olaf agreed, aware of the sharp look Paul sent his way.

Keith and Rob turned to them, faces wet and

flushed. They looked so different, it was hard to see they were brothers, and yet there was something similar about them.

Keith sniffed and turned to Olaf. "I'll never be able to thank you enough. And you, Paul. You've given me the world."

"You're welcome," Olaf said, a little hoarse himself. He drew Keith to one side. "Are you all right for us to leave you?"

"I am. Logan's on standby if we need him. Thank you." Keith shook Olaf's hand. "What do I owe you for today?"

Olaf rolled his eyes. "Paul would kill me if I charged you for being a friend. Go connect with your brother. And you know where I am if you need me."

"I do. And thank you again. I never thought I'd have this day."

Olaf drew Paul away, and they walked to their car. He glanced at Paul who sighed happily. "Well?"

"I never expected your first case as a private investigator to mean so much to me personally."

"I know what you mean. But not every case is like this. Look at Jace Comerford. He's getting a divorce."

"But at least he knows now that it isn't worth holding onto his marriage."

Olaf had discovered the ex in bed with another man. One photo, and Comerford started divorce proceedings.

Olaf's first cheating husband case had been messy. The only good thing that had come out of it was more work from Comerford himself. Once Comerford had discovered Olaf was an ex-cop, he put more work his way. Almost more work than he could handle. Olaf was looking forward to Paul finishing his notice period so he could start working full-time in the agency.

Thank goodness for Liam who had taken over the larger office above the Blue Lagoon as office manager while he did his masters part-time. Liam had a hidden talent for pursuing leads, so while Olaf did the legwork, Liam focused on the internet. Paul had yet to find his role, however, Olaf was sure Paul would tell him soon enough. Wig still complained when they met clients and leads in the restaurant but was mollified by the size of their coffee bill.

"I've got news for you, lover mine," Paul said.

"What's that?" Olaf was still musing about the new agency.

Paul beamed at him. "You are looking at the newest and brightest full-time partner of Skandik and Owens."

Olaf stopped and stared at him. "You're finished at the station?"

"Yep. The new inspector was free sooner than she thought, so I begged and made a nuisance of myself, and here I am." Paul leaned forwards. "All. Fucking. Yours."

Olaf's mouth went dry. "Fuck."

"Yes. Now."

Olaf raised an eyebrow. "You want me to throw you down on the sidewalk and fuck you here?"

"Pavement," Paul corrected. "And no. Take me

home. I'm going to cuff you to the bed and ride you until your brain dribbles out of your ears."

"God yes," Olaf said hoarsely.

They were stripping off their clothes almost before the front door was closed. By the time they reached the bedroom, they were naked and hard, cocks dripping in anticipation.

"Get on the bed," Paul ordered.

Olaf flung himself on the bed, made for once with clean sheets in anticipation of Paul's arrival, and put his hands over his head. Paul cuffed him to the frame with the ease of long practice. There was a key taped behind the bed that Olaf could reach, but unlocking the cuffs was an essential part of Paul's lovemaking. Olaf was a top. Always had been, always would be. And Paul, thank God, didn't complain that the chances he got to top were few and far between. But when Olaf was cuffed, Paul was in charge.

Paul locked gazes with him. "I get to see your beautiful body every day."

"It's really happening?" Olaf had waited for this moment for so long, he couldn't quite believe that Paul was now his.

"You. Me. Together. The flat has a new tenant in two weeks. I'm storing my gear at Mum and Dad's until we decide what we're doing."

Olaf knew this. He didn't care about the fine details. All he cared about was the fact his lover wasn't leaving him again.

Paul crawled up him, moaning as he rubbed his body over Olaf's fuzz. Olaf gasped as Paul swirled his tongue around the head of Olaf's cock.

Paul's moan was decadent. "You taste so good."

"Got to taste you," Olaf begged, desperate to swallow Paul to the root.

"Not yet, babe. This is my turn to love you." Paul licked and nibbled his way up the shaft.

"You're gonna be lucky if you get as far as riding me," Olaf grumbled.

Paul raised his head. "You're not to come until I say."

Olaf stared at him. "What?"

"You heard me. If you can make me come on demand, I can do the same for you."

Olaf got even harder at the growl in Paul's voice. It was a real turn on. "No coming. Right." He watched a pear-shaped drop ooze from the slit of his cock and run down the head, to be licked up by Paul's greedy tongue. "You're gonna kill me."

Paul's smile was positively wicked. "Not yet, Skandik."

The End

WANT TO READ ABOUT PAUL AND OLAF'S WEDDING DAY?

There came a point in every man's life where he had to put up or shut up. This was Olaf Skandik's moment. He stood in front of an island of Owenses, Gillards, Brents, and whatever Wig and Nibs called themselves. Half the island coppers were vying for space with the Met police force.

Even Paul's ex-Chief Superintendent had turned up with his daughter and a crate of chocolate sauce. Olaf had watched Paul nearly swallow his tongue when the Chief Super presented the gift from the Darrow nick. He had a feeling the man had waited a long time for that moment.

In the back was a row of people he'd never expected. Keith and Miriam Sargent, Rob and Jack, and Tony Dobson. Keith had called and asked if they could attend the wedding. Olaf wanted them there and Paul agreed. If it hadn't been for this case, he might never have been standing with Paul, the only man in the world who'd dragged him out of his cosy closet, kicking and screaming, to steal his heart.

He looked into his fiance's deep brown eyes, seeing the worry grow as Olaf didn't answer.

"I will," Olaf said, and Paul beamed at him.

"About bloody time."

Olaf rolled his eyes as everyone started laughing. He'd expected it from one of the Owens's brothers, but not from his new mother-in-law.

"What Mum said," Paul hissed.

Olaf raised an eyebrow. "Who was it who cancelled the last wedding?"

"There was another lockdown, dipshit," Paul snapped. "I wasn't getting married with six guests."

A polite cough reminded Olaf that they hadn't finished proceedings. They both turned to the registrar, who looked resigned. She'd married all the Owens boys and the extended clan. She was used to it.

"Sorry," Olaf said.

"Shall we proceed?"

"Yes," Paul agreed, then he frowned. "No, wait."

She shut her mouth.

"Paul, what's wrong?"

Now Olaf was worried. Paul had talked of nothing but the wedding for months, and now he was hesitating? Olaf was conscious of his parents and their spouses, and his siblings sitting in the front row. His siblings didn't care. They loved him. But even up to the previous night, even knowing Paul was his partner, his mother was trying to get him to change his mind and find a nice girl to settle down with and make baby Skandiks. He was never going to be able to live this down if Paul bailed on him now.

But Paul smiled at him. "Nothing, sweetheart."

Olaf breathed easier.

Paul wrapped his hands around Olaf's and pressed them against his heart. "Olaf Skandik, I just need to tell you that I love you and I can't believe we've got this far together."

Someone—Colin—muttered, "Nor can we."

But Olaf ignored him. "I love you too, and you're the only person I've ever wanted to take this journey with."

Paul's eyes filled with tears, and he sniffled. "Okay."

Olaf bent to kiss him.

"You're supposed to do that after the service,"

the registrar whispered.

Olaf felt Paul's wicked grin against his mouth, then Paul turned to her. "We've done it many, many times already. But we're ready."

But he didn't let go of Olaf's hands.

And finally, they were married. Olaf and Paul...there was some discussion going on about their surnames.

Their wedding started with the same music that Liam and Sam had used. Alex's beautiful voice in the room had given it gravitas, and it had been part of Olaf's first introduction to the family. It was Liam's gift, with Tea's and Kathy's approval. They left with Billy Idol's *White Wedding*, because, of course, it was Paul.

Then they were surrounded by family and friends, hugging, and kissing him. He was passed from one Owens to another until he didn't know who he'd hugged, and finally he was in front of his parents.

"Mom. Dad."

His mother glanced at his father and then back at him. "I thought I could persuade you to come home."

"I *am* home, Mom." He'd called the Isle of Wight home for five years now, and while he missed his family, he'd never been happier.

"I can see that."

"We both can," his father assured him, and he was eased by his father's acceptance. He knew it hadn't been easy for either of them to come to terms with Olaf's relationship with Paul. Especially because it was Paul. "And you have a family here too."

Olaf turned and saw Paul, surrounded by his brothers, giving him a worried look. He smiled and Paul relaxed a fraction. Olaf knew Paul was ready to come over and do battle for him if he needed it. "They're overwhelming at times, but I couldn't ask for a better family to marry into."

He was forty-six and finally he had everything he desired.

"Congratulations, Ollie." His sister flung her arms around him.

"Don't call me Ollie," he said automatically.

Sarah ignored him of course. "It's time you introduced us to everyone."

"Are you sure you're ready for it?" he murmured.

She looked down her nose at him. "I'm a Skandik. I'm ready for anything."

He hugged her close to him. "I love you, big sis."

"I love you too."

"Put him down, Sarah. You don't know where he's been."

Olaf grinned at his stepbrother over his sister's head. "Thanks, Lucas."

"You're welcome."

He enfolded Lucas into a hug. Although they weren't related by blood, his stepbrother was built like him with the same tall, rangy frame and white-blond hair. Then he stepped back to see the gay men from the island staring at them with their mouths open, including his husband.

"Scandinavian porn," Cam muttered.

"Behave," he mouthed, then he rolled his eyes at their mock-innocent looks.

Paul at least was honest. "Not a chance."

"Should I ask?" Lucas asked.

"No," Olaf assured him hastily. "You really don't want to ask."

Lucas turned to look at the guys now pretending not to watch them. "Good looking guys."

Olaf's jaw dropped open. "You're not…"

"You can say the word, Ollie," Lucas teased. "The parents won't spontaneously combust."

"Have you met my mother? And don't call me Ollie. You haven't answered the question."

"No, I'm not gay. But I can appreciate a good-looking man. The bear is yummy."

Bear? Olaf furrowed his brow. "Oh, Nibs. Yeah, he's very taken, and Wig will have you by the balls if you lay a finger on him."

"Who's Wig?"

"One guess."

"The short flaming dude?"

"Right first time. He's the scariest of the bunch."

"We could just say hello instead of staring at them," Sarah suggested.

Olaf looked between the two of them. "I'm so glad you're here. Really glad." He hauled them into another hug.

"Aw, Ollie's getting all emotional," Sarah teased. "Let go of me, you ape."

Olaf did, but not before he'd ruffled Sarah's hair.

He introduced his siblings to his adopted family and grinned as they learnt what it was like to become an Owens.

Olaf heard a cough. He turned to see Keith and Miriam, Rob and Jack, plus Tony who looked as if his world had fallen apart.

"I'm glad you're here," he said honestly, shaking their hands.

He held onto Tony's hand. "How are you?"

"Shite," Tony admitted. "But getting there."

The fallout from Tony's revelation that he was gay had been messy. His wife threw him out of the house, and his kids refused to talk to him. But the island boys stepped up on Olaf's request. Tony now lived in Cameron's old house, and he was discovering what it was like to be adopted by the Owenses and Gillards. It turned out Kim worked with Nick's mum, and Sara and Charley and Mattie made sure she wasn't forgotten. No one got left behind on this island. His kids refused to have anything to do with them, but Olaf had hope that maybe one day they would forgive their dad.

Tony was still struggling with the fact his friend was alive. He was angry and resentful that Bobby had gone off to have a long, happy marriage with Jacob, while fear had forced Tony down a path he'd never wanted. But they were talking, so maybe there was hope.

Then they were replaced by Nick and Logan and Sara, and Olaf stopped thinking about his first case to be engulfed in hugs with his friends. He was so damn lucky.

Later in the evening at Rose's cottage, when it was just their families and the guys, Paul leaned against him as they watched Sarah talk animatedly with Colin, Fee, Dan, and Tea, and Lucas get absorbed into a long discussion with Nibs, Jeff, Cam, Logan, and Nick about steak, of all things.

"I guess the Owenses have two more adopted into their family," Paul murmured.

Olaf looked down at his love. "I should tell them to run."

Paul beamed at him. "Too late."

Olaf wrapped his arms around Paul and watched the families mix. His parents were enfolded in a group of older Owenses and Gillards.

"Happy, lover?" Paul asked.

"I can't quite believe it."

"You. Me. Our wedding day?"

Olaf buried his nose into Paul's hair, inhaling the fresh citrus scent of his shampoo. "I'm finally married to the man of my dreams."

"You're gonna make my mascara run."

"Nothing makes you cry," Olaf pointed out, not commenting on the fact Paul was wearing a touch of mascara. He'd seen Fee and Tea flapping around Paul earlier.

It also wasn't quite true that Paul never cried. He'd seen Paul fall apart over cases at work, particularly ones that involved kids. But, day to day, Paul was more likely to laugh than cry.

"So does Lucas have the fuzz all over like you do?" Paul murmured.

"We're not related," Olaf pointed out. "He's my

stepbrother."

"I know." And there was heat behind Paul's words.

"No," Olaf said firmly.

"No to the fuzz?"

"No to the lewd thoughts about me and my brother in bed together."

"With me too," Paul pointed out.

"No," he said firmly. Because *hell* no.

"Spoilsport."

Olaf counted to ten in Swedish, and then ten more because he'd just learned that.

"Gotcha," Paul said, a wicked glint in his eye.

Also by Sue Brown

STANDALONE books
Summer's Dawn | Summer's Song | A Tale Told in Darkness | A Cock in the Window | In-Decision | The Backpack | The Clumsy Santa | Mr Plum | Chance to Be King | Made for Aaron | Final Admission | The Layered Mask | The Next Call | The Night Porter | Light of Day | The Sky Is Dead | Nothing Ever Happens | Stolen Dreams | Waiting | Prey Time | Louis Hates Valentines Day | Racing Raindrops | The Fireman's Pole Falling for Ramos | Last Place at the Chalet | Snow Twink | Winter Prince

JT'S BAR series
His Shield | His Guardian | His Warrior | His Valentine | His Protector | His Sentinel | His Defender

BIKER DADDY BODYGUARDS
Hold Firm | Hold Close | Hold Safe | Hold Tight

ANGEL ENTERPRISES series
Morning My Angel | Goodnight My Angel | Hello

My Angel

LYON ROAD VETS series
Hairy Harry's Car Seat | Bob, the Destroyer of Leads | Hazel Takes Over | Stormin' Norman | Lyon Road Vets Boxset

COWBOYS AND ANGELS series
Speed Dating the Boss | Secretly Dating the Lionman | Slow Dating the Detective

WITH A KICK series (with Clare London)
Hissed as a Newt | Bells and Balls

FRANKIE'S series
Frankie & Al | Ed & Marchant | Anthony & Leo | Jordan & Rhys |

THE ISLE series
The Isle of... Where? | Isle of Wishes | Isle of Waves | Isle of Waiting | Island Doctor | Island Counsellor | Island Detective

MORNING REPORT series
Morning Report | Complete Faith | Go-to Guy | Luke's Present | Letters From a Cowboy |

About Sue Brown

Cranky middle-aged author with an addiction for coffee, and a passion for romancing two guys. She loves her dog, she loves her kids, and she loves coffee; in which order very much depends on the time of day.

Come over and talk to Sue at:
Newsletter: http://bit.ly/SueBrownNews
Bookbub: https://www.bookbub.com/profile/sue-brown
Patreon: https://www.patreon.com/suebrownstories
Website: http://www.suebrownstories.com/
Facebook group: https://www.facebook.com/SueBrownsStories/
Email: sue@suebrownstories.com

Milton Keynes UK
Ingram Content Group UK Ltd.
UKHW030238030224
437175UK00001B/35